INTRIGUED BY DESIRE

A Raising the Stakes Novella:

Book One

By: Chantele Belamour

Chapter One: A Rough Start

"Dang it!" Lucy yelled as she opened her eyes to see the alarm clock flashing "12:00 AM", even though she could see the sunlight coming through the window.

She looked at her phone to see it was "8:00AM" and there were two missed calls, three texts, and a voice message. The first message said "Where are you?", the second sent ten minutes later "Hellllोooo your shift started two hours ago!!!", and the third " You better have a damn good excuse for why I'M still here two hours after MY shift ended" which was followed by a pissed off emoji. After the last message she didn't even want to hear whatever had been left on the voice message.

Shit was definitely going to hit the fan when she got there. If it wasn't bad enough the power had gone out in the middle of the night her phone was on silent, and she had forgotten to set any of the alarms on her phone. Oh, and said phone was on 15% because the USB cord wasn't plugged into the charger so even if the power hadn't gone out her phone still wouldn't have charged. What a great way to begin the morning. Might as well take a shower since I'm already late she muttered to herself as she pulled her red work shirt out of the closet, ransacked the top drawer to find a pair of black workpants and grabbed some undergarments and socks out of the next drawer.

Ten minutes later she emerged, hurriedly threw some gel and mousse in her curly hair and threw it up into a ponytail. There was no time to diffuse it so, it was up to fate if her curls would look good after they finished airdrying. After brushing her teeth, putting on deodorant, and spraying on her favorite Vera's Secret perfume she was finally ready to go. Fifteen minutes later she was turning into the parking lot so quickly her tires screeched as she barely avoided running into the giant neon orange Sunset Paradise Resort sign at the entrance. The last thing I need this morning is to crash my car and get fired she thought as she parked and exited the car in a rush.

As soon as she got into the building, she could almost feel the red-hot heat of her coworker Diane's eyes zeroing in on her.

As she walked into the gift shop Diane angrily whispered "It's about damn time you showed up I was supposed to pick my kids up from the babysitters house three hours ago. I had to call the babysitter to say I'd be late for pickup and now it's going to cost me 40 extra dollars, which I don't have, all because somebody wanted to get some extra beauty rest this morning. Luckily MY replacement showed up on time, so I was able to open the gift shop for you."

Diane was the night auditor, but she did occasionally pick up a shift or two in the gift shop which came in handy when someone called off or showed up late. Lucy reached into her purse and pulled out two twenties as she tried to explain she was sorry her power had gone out, her phone was on silent, and her alarms weren't set.

The money seemed to calm Diane a bit, but that didn't stop her from sarcastically commenting "Luckily Matt isn't going to be here today so he doesn't know you're late, but even if he did, you'd just flash him those brown doe eyes and he'd probably forget all about it since he's got a thing for you."

Lucy hated to admit it, but Diane wasn't lying. Matt's feelings for her were obvious to everyone who worked there.

Chapter Two: My Life in Shadow Ridge

Luckily, it was a slow day with less than a hundred people in house so the hours would go by slowly, but at least hopefully she wouldn't have any customers screaming at her today. The gift shop she worked at was in between the lobby and the full-service restaurant which served a buffet for breakfast. Often times people would make remarks about how wrong it was, that they were forced to walk through the toy section on their way to get their food.

However, the actual entrance to the breakfast buffet was on the far side of the gift shop near the elevators and there were signs pointing towards breakfast so walking through the gift shop wasn't a requirement. Either way, it's not as if she was the one who designed the place so there was nothing she could do about the placement, and she certainly wasn't grabbing them by the ear and dragging them in to spend their hard-earned dollars. Just then, as if on cue a group of people walked through and one of the toddlers started to reach for a small stuffed animal on a table.

She heard the person whom she assumed was the mother of the toddler mutter to herself "great now I'm going to have to come back in and buy that overpriced toy or there's going to be a meltdown."

She smiled as the guests walked by hoping maybe the child would forget about the toy so later the lady wouldn't feel obligated to scold her for putting the toy in the child's line of sight.

On a normal day Lucy found waking up at five in the morning to get ready for work no fun to begin with, but being reprimanded by an irritated customer on a day she was late would make this day worse. Besides getting up before most the birds started moving around in their nests, the job wasn't bad. Her usual work hours were 6am-3pm so at least she had a few hours after work to relax and unwind before repeating this process four days a week, and up to six during a busy season. Even during the slower months when her off days were Tuesday thru Thursday, her pay was still enough to pay all the bills at her small apartment plus the typical groceries.

Shadow Ridge was a very small town in Southern Indiana so there weren't many job opportunities that paid above minimum wage. She had lived here her entire life, and while the town had grown significantly since her childhood it was still a small town. The population was less than 2,000 people. Besides the medium size hotel she worked at there were two small gas stations, two fast food places, a Mexican restaurant, a Chinese restaurant, a pizza place, a grocery store, a 24/7 breakfast restaurant, two small hotels, the town library, a popular bowling alley with an indoor go cart track, Mini golf, and a lazar tag place that was two stories tall that was owned by a famous former basketball player named Larry Hawk, and a large casino which was just outside the town limits in the next town over.

There used to be a small family-owned drive-in movie theater, but it had closed down a few years ago due to low revenue. The nostalgia townsfolk had, simply couldn't keep up with the changing times. People were able to pay to watch movies that were still in theaters via streaming apps from the comfort of their homes.

Customer service wasn't a glamorous occupation, but at twenty Lucy still had time to go back to college if she wanted to. She had taken a few basic classes at the community college a few towns over, but nothing had felt like "her true calling". Instead of going into massive debt while trying to figure it out, for now she was content with making enough money to have a car and a place of her own. Her car was a used 2007 Pontilac Vibe with 130,000 miles which wasn't too bad considering it was only 5 grand which over the 24-month loan period only added up to a little over $250 a month and with insurance it was around $340.

Most of her days in the gift shop were spent folding shirts, returning items to their proper places, and wiping down every surface at least five times. Now that might sound boring to some people, but as an introvert it wasn't the worst job to have when conversational skills weren't a strong suit. Besides seating the occasional person for lunch and asking guests if they needed help finding souvenirs there wasn't much beyond small talk required of her.

Her coworkers were friendly enough, but the only one she saw outside of work was Jaden, who also happened to be her best friend. They had been friends since middle school. Lucy who was normally quiet and non-confrontational had thrown a punch at Rachel Kingsley, the most popular girl in school for calling the new student a gay slur. She got detention, but it was worth it to teach that hoity toity not to be a homophobe. Jaden had ended up in detention too because a teacher overheard him call Rachel a word that rhymed with witch. Not that she didn't deserve it, but profanity in school was an automatic detention. Conveniently no teachers had been around to hear what Rachel had said. Still even if they had, Rachel wouldn't have gotten in any trouble because her parents were filthy rich and donated money to the school every year.

In detention they had bonded over the fact that neither one of them felt like they fit in with other people in town. Since she was in elementary school she had dealt with subtle and sometimes overt racism as a result of being one of the only black people in Shadow Ridge. Indiana may have been part of the Union, but it certainly felt like a lot of Shadow Ridge's citizens were convinced it had been part of the Confederacy. Jaden confided in her that his family had moved to Shadow Ridge from a small southern town in Texas after student's aka bullies at his last school had vandalized his locker after finding out he was gay. She didn't have much experience in the area, but from what she had seen on tv and what he told her school could be tough for gay teens. Especially ones without a supportive family, which was why statistics showed that many people would wait until after graduating to tell anyone.

Hopefully someday times would change and people would be free to be as out and proud as Jaden without the threat of judgy bigots. Luckily Jaden's family was supportive so he had been comfortable enough to tell them. The school system however didn't share the same sentiments and had refused to suspend the students responsible so his parents thought a fresh start might help. Thus, even though there were no fond memories of high school for either of them at least they had found a sense of comradery.

Without Jaden there to keep her company the day seemed to drag on and on until finally after the hundredth time she looked at the clock it was 2:55. Hopefully her replacement wouldn't be late which was a bit ironic considering that she'd been late herself. Fortunately, the guest from earlier hadn't said anything when she came back in and bought the toy so at least her workday wasn't going to end as bad as her day had started. Her replacement Molly showed up a few minutes later. At the end of her workday the last thing she had to do was run a cashier's report and count down her bank. This report would show her how much money she had to deposit and put into the drop envelope. As long as the cash amount and her bank were both correct things would be good.

Sometimes there were computer errors that happened such as the previous day's reports running together, or transactions being voided incorrectly but those events rarely occurred. It wasn't a huge deal as long as she let Matt know and wrote a note on the drop envelope so it could be investigated further. Everything checked out so she filled out the drop envelope and deposited it in the bank room. Now she was officially free to go home and enjoy the rest of her day.

Chapter Three: A Normal Evening

Upon arriving home Lucy realized that she hadn't eaten anything all day, so she looked in the freezer and found some frozen Generals Tso's chicken and some shrimp fried rice. After heating the oven to 400°F she threw the chicken in and set the timer to go off in 25 minutes so she could mix the sauce in. The rice was the steam in a bag kind, that takes a few minutes in the microwave, so she'd wait until the last few minutes before the chicken was done to throw it in.

While she waited, she searched through a few streaming apps until she found an episode of a cooking competition to watch. It was called Ruthless Kitchen, and it was hosted by a famous food connoisseur named Anton Grey. Contestants were each given 50,000 to spend on different sabotages during the competition. After each round, a famous guest unaware of any potential sabotages would judge how close the contestants had met the assigned food criteria and eliminate whoever failed the assignment. In the final round the last two contestants would have a final showdown, and the winner would leave with whatever money they hadn't spent. Right before the winner was announced she heard the timer go off so she paused it and got up to mix in the sauce and steam the rice.

After setting the microwave timer to five minutes, Lucy grabbed a plate from the cabinet and some utensils from the silverware drawer and set them on the countertop which also functioned as her kitchen table since the apartment wasn't big enough for a whole table set. While she waited for the microwave to beep and indicate her rice was done, she ventured back into the front room to finish the episode. Oh of course the one contestant she'd been rooting against had won and taken home 20,000 which was less than half the money but quite the hefty sum for a 24-year-old line cook with barely any experience compared to the older contestants which had included an executive chef at a fancy restaurant in Hollywood. Right after the message 'play next episode' appeared at the bottom of the screen she heard the microwave go off.

Instructions on the back of the bag had said she needed to give the rice a minute to stand so that she wouldn't get burned by the steam emitting. Time to pull the chicken out and let it rest for a minute before piling it onto the plate. It should be safe now to carefully open the side of the bag that had a green arrow pointing to the words 'open this side only'. Half the bag should do for tonight I'll save the rest for leftovers or maybe a midnight snack she thought as she carefully poured some rice onto her plate. After grabbing some chicken, she was finally ready to dig in and quiet the loud rumbling her stomach had been doing while she was waiting for the food to get done. The food was tasty, but it just wasn't the same as it was at The Flaming Wok! her favorite local Chinese Restaurant. After she finished eating and watching a few more episodes of Ruthless Kitchen it was getting late.

Before she headed to bed she needed to put the rest of the food in the fridge. Once she had finished that task it was time to use the bathroom and brush her teeth. There was nothing worse than waking up in the middle of a perfectly good dream and racing to the restroom half asleep with a full bladder. Well other than the thought of realizing midway through an outfit change that the curtains were open just enough that anybody walking by would get a free peep show. After making sure that the curtains were properly closed, she grabbed a pajama set from her drawers. Was she too old for purple pj's with cutesy penguins on them? Maybe, but it's not as if anyone else was going to see them.

There wasn't really a need to spend $50 on a lingerie set at Vera's Secret when men weren't fighting each other over the right to ask her out let alone to get into her pants. Not that she had any "real" dating experience or actual knowledge of what to do if they did for some reason want to sleep with her. She wasn't totally clueless because of health classes and movies on TV where couples simulated passionately getting down to business, but watching fictional couples and actually being face to face with someone in the heat of the moment were sure to be two different things.

As far as dating went there had only been Derek, in eighth grade for all of two weeks which is when she had heard him by his locker bragging to his friends that he was "this close to getting some". Boy was he embarrassed when she marched over and informed his friends that the only thing that he was close to getting was a kick in the balls for lying. To save face he'd broken up with her on the spot and said, "as if I'd want to sleep with a weirdo like you anyways." He hadn't elaborated on what he felt had qualified her as a weirdo, but after that display of immaturity she didn't care what he thought of her anymore. 6 years later the only thing she regretted was wasting her first kiss on such a revolting person and the fact that she was currently revisiting this memory instead of sleeping. After setting the alarm clock next to her bed for 5 AM and checking her phone alarms twice for good measure she finally closed her eyes and drifted off to sleep.

Chapter Four:

Breakfast, Lunch, And Karens

In the morning when her alarm clock started ringing, she opened one eye in annoyance to see the red flashing "5:00 AM". At least she was going to be on time this morning, but as usual she had woken up right in the middle of a dream. The details of the dream were fuzzy, but there was definitely a guy with his face obscured, and they were somewhere by the sea or maybe an ocean. Maybe her brain had conjured up a forgotten image from a history book or a piece of art she'd seen somewhere. If that was the case though, why did she wake up feeling like she was somehow connected to both the place and this mysterious shadowy figure. Lying in bed pondering what the dream meant wasn't going to help with getting to work on time, so she got up and started her daily routine.

A package of mini chocolate chip muffins would have to do for breakfast. Not the healthiest choice, but it's not like there was time to construct a three-course menu. Besides they were pretty tasty. Next was a quick trip to the restroom, followed by laying out work clothes, then back to the bathroom to brush the ol' teeth and fix the ponytail if necessary. A spritz of perfume and deodorant application later and she was finally ready to put on her work clothes and shoes.

Twenty minutes later, which is the time it usually took when she wasn't driving like a speed demon the way she had the previous day, she pulled into the parking lot with ten minutes to spare before her shift started. After parking and making a final check to be sure she had her ID badge, bank key, and card to get into the bank room she was ready to head inside. "Well look who decided to show up to work on time today " Diane said as Lucy walked past the reservation counter. She knew Diane was just joking, so she decided to play along, " I know, how am I ever going to win worst employee of the month if I only show up late once?" They both laughed at that because there were so many new employees constantly in and out of the place that Diane, Lucy, and Jaden all referred to new schedules as "the first draft." It was almost a guarantee that as soon as it was posted someone was going to quit, call in, or get fired by the next day.

Working customer service was certainly no walk in the park, but considering new hires were making at least $12 an hour it wasn't a money issue. Even though it was almost a seasonal job people could cross train in other departments to get hours even when the restaurant and gift shop were closed midweek during slow times. Housekeepers deep cleaned on those days and the hotel itself was still open throughout the week so front desk personnel got their hours in. Some people just didn't like to work and their lifestyle somehow accommodated this. Maybe they had rich friends or relatives secretly funneling money into their accounts. However they were achieving this unemployed lifestyle it simply wasn't an option for her.

Although it was only 7AM she could already tell it was going to be a busy Saturday. The amount of cars in the parking lot when she pulled up was a good indication to guesstimate how many guests had stayed overnight. She walked over to the host stand and saw that the paper said 375 which wasn't the worst, but it was definitely going to be busy.

There were no servers in the morning just a host, buffet attendant, and a few bussers depending on if it was the weekend or a school day. On the weekends most of the staff were high schoolers trying to make a little extra cash to pay for cars and going out on dates. Even so, they were only slightly more reliable than the adult workers that would come and go. There were sports or band schedules, and family events that all had to be worked around. Additionally, fifteen- and sixteen-year-olds would rather spend their weekends hanging out with friends, so sometimes they would call in to spend just to spend time being teenagers.

The restaurant was open from 7AM-10AM and served a full hot breakfast buffet with sausage links, ham slices, scrambled eggs, biscuits, gravy, and hashbrowns. On the cold bar along with the white milk and orange juice, yogurt and hard-boiled eggs were available. Despite the fact that it was included with the guests overnight stay sometimes people would still be upset that there weren't pancakes, waffles, and bacon on the buffet. Guests had access to the soda machine as well, but lack of chocolate milk was an issue. Especially since when she first started at the hotel it had been offered. Matt had stopped ordering though due to the amount of people who would take 5 or more with them after finishing breakfast.

Cases of chocolate milk were twice as expensive and combined with the number of cases of white milk that would expire and be thrown away it wasn't good for food costs. At first due to comment cards asking for it to come back he decided to compromise and still order 2 or 3 cases and offer it for sale in the gift shop cooler along with apple juice and flavorade. However, unlike the apple juice which people begrudgingly paid for, people rarely bought the chocolate milk so it would expire. After a few times of this happening, he stopped ordering it again.

Since arriving for her shift, she had already straightened up the gift shop, folded the t-shirts, wiped the counters and other surfaces down so there was nothing more for her to do at the moment. It was nearing 8AM and the line for breakfast was starting to get long. Currently there were no customers in the gift shop, so she went over to help the hostess, Sarah. It wasn't something that was required for her to do, but it certainly helped things move smoother with two people. One person could mark off the room numbers and keep track of how many guests had been through so the kitchen could keep up with how much food to put out. The other person could seat guests at tables and explain to them where their food, drinks, and trashcans were. Having two people at the hostess stand also helped with stopping guests from trying to seat themselves or walking in without shirts and shoes on. Matt seemed to think that the two signs in glass frames on the wall and a laminated sign on the front of the hostess stand that said, "shoes and shirts are required," would stop them, but people would still argue that it was a stupid rule.

There was also a standing sign right next to the hostess stand that listed all the available food choices and at the very top in black 48 bold print said, "please wait to be seated" and a laminated sign on the hostess stand as well, but some people would still try to ignore it. Sometimes guests would get so angry at having to do both of these things that Lucy would have to call the front desk manager over to speak with them. They'd try to argue or give dirty looks but 8 out of 10 times they would just admit defeat and go on their way because they wanted that free food.

On holiday weekends and during the summer the hotel would stay at or near total capacity of 500. Trying to get 500 people in and out in three hours on those days was stressful on the person at the host stand. Those days the restaurant would completely fill up and there would still be a line of people waiting and getting angry that they couldn't be seated. To keep track of which tables had already been seated the host or hostess would place white coasters that had guests room numbers written on them so they could return to the correct table after grabbing their food. People waiting in line would point to "empty tables" they could physically see, but Sarah would explain that people in line were coming back to these tables. During the times there were no tables Sarah would do what she could by taking down room numbers and calling them out as soon as the bussers could get a table clean. The other option was offering to go boxes for people who preferred to get their food and go instead of waiting for a table and then in the food line.

For the amount of people in house today things were moving along alright. Just over 150 people had been through and there weren't many people left in line at the moment. When 9AM hit things would be completely different though. The last hour was always congested because everyone left would come down at once severely underestimating the fact that other folks on vacation like to sleep in too. The line wasn't very long so Sarah would be able to manage by herself for now.

Lucy stepped back over to the gift shop just as a family was approaching the gift shop counter. She put on a big smile and greeted them while asking if they had found everything alright. When she was finished ringing them up, she told them to have a great day, and they went happily on their way. After cashing out a few more people she noticed the breakfast line was starting to get long again and it looked like there were only two or three tables left. Sarah was definitely going to need help taking down room numbers in a few minutes if the line kept growing. As Sarah sat one of the remaining tables, she noticed that almost 200 people had been through. The bussers were cleaning off some tables now so hopefully most of this line could get in fairly quick.

Around the 250 mark there were no tables left and there was only 45 minutes left. There were a few grumbles as Sarah started telling people that they could wait for a table or get to go containers, but most people could see that it wasn't her fault, so they waited patiently for her to get them in. By 9:45 everyone who had been in line waiting had been seated. At 10AM Sarah closed the gate and put out the sign that said, "Sorry Restaurant is closed." Anyone who arrived after 10, but before the buffet was taken down when the last people left could get to go boxes, but they couldn't sit down.

Occasionally this would displease some folks, but it's not like they were being refused breakfast altogether. If people chose to forgo free breakfast altogether simply because they couldn't sit down, then that was their choice. As Jaden would say, "it's not my problem if some people can't get out of bed in time when they have three whole hours to come down here." When Jaden and Lucy had first started working at the hotel two and a half years ago there were servers during breakfast, but that had been phased out during their first six months. Servers were always calling in or quitting, and it was cheaper on the company to just hire a few teens to bus from 8am-1pm.As a result, Jaden had switched from being a breakfast server to an afternoon server so his shifts were from 12pm-10pm.

The restaurant closed at 9pm, but he never got out of the place at exactly 9 because there was still side work that needed to be done before leaving for the night. Vacuuming, rolling silverware, and restocking condiments might not sound like it would take too long after closing, but that was assuming that all the tables were gone and the servers could start cleaning right at close.

This almost never happened because there always seemed to be a last-minute table of six that would walk in at 8:55 and order whatever items took the longest to cook. These customers drove Jaden crazy because they were usually the messiest tables and they'd always stick around way after closing talking the night away. Rolling silverware and restocking condiments could get done during that time, but company policy was very clear on the fact that vacuuming couldn't be started until all customers were gone. Which is why servers were scheduled until 10 to account for any cleaning that needed to be done afterwards. However, the way the floors looked after a busy morning or night it was usually at least an hour for one person to vacuum properly. Despite having three vacuums only one ever seemed to be in working condition.

Now that the breakfast rush was over it was time for Lucy to straighten up the gift shop. There were always t-shirts to refold, toys discarded on the floor by children, and items to move back to their correct displays. Of course, she knew it was her job to put the things back where they belonged, but was it too really too much to ask of grown adults not to haphazardly throw the t-shirts back onto the shelf. Although there were four neon colors to choose from the design on all the shirts were exactly the same. The hotel name in black cursive font in between two lime green palm trees, an elementary school style sun in the corner, and a few dark blue squiggles at the bottom representing waves people would still unfold all the shirts as if the design was going to magically change from color to color.

There could be an argument made about people unfolding them to look at the sizes, but there was one in every available size (on child and adult size mannequins) hanging up along the wall with labels underneath indicating the sizes. No matter the reason, it was just frustrating neatly refolding the shirts only to see them in disarray five minutes later. She had almost finished with the current round of refolding when Matt walked into the gift shop. Immediately her mind started racing trying to figure out if he was just walking through or if the dreaded writeup was coming. Inexplicably her entire body felt as though it was simultaneously on fire and ice cold. Despite this she managed to squeak out a hello as if everything was totally fine. Hopefully he wouldn't be able to detect how "not fine" she was actually feeling.

Matt must've smelled the sense of dread rolling off her because the first thing he said he said was, " Don't worry Brown Eyes, I'm not going to write you up for a first-time offense, just don't let it become a habit, or I will be forced to take swift action. I can't have my best employee setting a bad example for the others."

Matt hardly ever called her Lucy, "Brown Eyes" had been his nickname for her since the moment he hired her. Was it slightly unprofessional for a boss to give a nickname to a female employee he obviously had feelings for? Yes, but he'd never done anything to make her fearful of him, or to indicate her job would be on the line for unreturned feelings. About a year ago he had asked her if she wanted to grab a bite to eat after work, but when she gently turned him down, he had never brought it up again.

Although she didn't personally find him attractive there were a few other co-workers she knew of that did. She didn't know his exact height, but he was probably around 5'10 with a slender but toned build, and hazel eyes. At 26, he was on the younger side compared to most of the other business owners in town, but apparently, he had inherited the hotel, a significant amount of money, a decent sized house and 10 acres of land after his grandparents who raised him had both passed away about 5 years ago.

From what she had heard secondhand through the grapevine his parents had tragically passed in a housefire when he was only a child. For obvious reasons he had never talked about his parents and it's not like that was the sort of thing that would ever randomly come up during a general work conversation. Now that the fear of being written up was gone she could go on about her day as usual.

"It was definitely just a one-time occurrence. Punctuality is very important to me," Lucy responded.

"Now that we have this matter resolved is there anything that I need to reorder for the giftshop? In a few weeks Summer break will be upon us and I expect it to be very busy again this year."

Taking a quick glance around, she mentioned a few toys and toiletries that were selling well. T-shirts would need to be reordered too because as much as she hated folding them the shirts were a hot ticket item and it sometimes it felt like forever before the new shipments would arrive. Matt was constantly having to look up the order dates and call the company for updates. She didn't quite understand why he put up with that, but she could only assume he must be either getting a really awesome deal or his grandparents had signed a lifetime contract with them.

"Alrighty, I'll put in that order as soon as I go back to my office. But first I'm going to get the kitchen to cook me a big ol' buffalo chicken wrap and some bacon cheddar fries."

That actually sounded pretty tasty. Maybe she'd order one for herself later. It was nice that employees had the option to sign and have $4.00 taken out of their checks for a meal instead of having to leave and risk wasting their entire break waiting for food elsewhere.

The list was comprised of 9 meal choices which wasn't too bad especially since the portion sizes were decent. If someone was to ask what her favorite meal on the list was it would be nearly impossible to decide between the buffalo style chicken wrap with fries and a buffalo cheeseburger and onion rings. Some people found it very strange that she would order her burger without onions, but then get onion rings as a side. The only explanation she could come up with was raw onions had a pungent taste, and cooked onions didn't.

Jaden's favorite items were the fish sandwich with house made chips and the tenderloin sandwich with curly fries. The tenderloin sandwich was by far the best seller in the restaurant, mainly because it was a gigantic fried pork patty that came fully dressed on a toasted bun. There was no denying that it was tasty, but she preferred beef over pork. Employees could also order food off the regular restaurant menu and get a 25% discount. Every once in a while, she would order a Mushroom Swiss Burger and fries which wasn't included in the employee meal choices, so the discount came in handy.

The food prices on the regular menu weren't actually that bad to begin with though. Appetizers were $5-8 which included Mozzarella Sticks, Fried Green Tomatoes, Chips and Salsa or Queso, Loaded Potato Skins, and Fried Pickle Spears. The burger choices were The Classic Hamburger/Cheeseburger, BBQ Bacon, Mushroom Swiss, Turkey, and Veggie, all of which were 1/3lb and ranged between $7-10 dollars. Basket choices were Chicken Strips, Fried Fish, Fried Shrimp, Boneless Wings, and Battered Mushrooms which ranged between $6-9. The wings could be ordered regular, or tossed in buffalo, BBQ, or honey mustard. Both the burgers and baskets were served with a choice of fries (crinkle cut or curly) and for an extra 1.50 bacon bits and cheddar could be added, house made chips, or onion rings. For a .75 up-charge people could pick one of the 7 other side choices which were coleslaw, rice pilaf, corn, mashed potatoes, side salad, steamed broccoli, and mac and cheese.

There were also fried or grilled chicken sandwiches, fried fish, and the tenderloin sandwich which were between $6-9. For people who preferred a healthier meal choice there was the veggie burger or large salads (regular or Caesar style) which for a $3 upcharge could be modified to include grilled chicken, salmon, or shrimp. The choice of kid's meal items which was limited compared to the rest of the menu were all $7, and consisted of mini burgers (2), hot dog, grilled cheese, mini corndogs, or chicken nuggets. All kids' meals included a free small drink, and the choice of fries, a fruit cup, or applesauce as the side.

Thinking about all the tasty items on the menu was fun, but there was still work to do and she better get back to it. Right as she was in the middle of wiping down the shelves and displays at the back of the store for the tenth time of the day, she heard a loud, drawn out and very irritated "Heeeeellllllllllooooooo" coming from the front of the store. Five seconds ago, when she had looked there was no one in the store and now this person was acting like she'd kept them waiting for half a century.

"Sorry just one second and I'll be right up there to help you " she called out. Not that giving an acknowledgement was going to help.

Judging by the tone she could tell that this interaction was likely going to be an unpleasant one. Oh, great the lady was also leaned halfway over her register as if she'd been taking a nap behind the register or something. She walked to the register as fast as possible to not keep her waiting any longer.

As expected, her cheery smile and usual greeting was met with a sneer and a tone. "Enlighten me, where are the toiletries located in this stupid overpriced shop?" It wasn't exactly a lie that things were probably overpriced, but then again, this was a hotel giftshop so of course things could be found cheaper elsewhere.

Hopefully the item she was looking for was even in the giftshop because clearly, she was in no mood to be told to drive to another store. "If you'll please follow me, I'll show you where all the toiletries are located." The toiletries were on a black wire display so she could have easily pointed to it, but it was probably in her best interest to be extra helpful to avoid any further issues.

"For cripes sake! Do I look like I am incapable of finding it all on my own. Just point me in the direction of the damn display you incompetent buffoon." Hopefully her customer service smile was still plastered on her face because she definitely didn't want the sting of that last comment to be obvious.

She used "the mouse mascot point" which was two fingers (index and middle finger) to point in the direction of the display. Pointing with one finger was commonly seen as rude and no way was, she going to risk being rude. The two finger point being seen as friendly was something she'd seen once on one those articles about "fun facts" of being employed by the most well-known international theme park. She wasn't sure if it was true, but customers had never complained about it.

Suddenly she heard loud muttering, well shouting was more accurate of "1.99 is highway robbery for a toothbrush that is provided for free in every other hotel on the planet." However, the price didn't stop the lady from begrudgingly heading back up to the counter with the toothbrush in hand. As she started to ring up the item she could sense that this interaction wasn't going to end with the transaction.

"I demand to speak to your manager so I can ask why they have such incompetent employees pricing these toothbrushes like they are made of 24 carat gold." Lucy was baffled by the comparison since paying $1.99 was far from the price of gold, but she definitely was not going to voice that thought.

She handed the lady back her change and got out the phone to call Matt's office extension.

When he picked up the phone, she used her friendliest voice to say "Mr. Campbell there is a customer who wishes to speak to you immediately." She knew Matt wouldn't even both asking what it was regarding because he knew that when she spoke in that particular voice it meant that no additional info could be given because the customer was irate and probably glaring daggers at her.

She could tell from the unnatural 'cat that ate the canary' grin stretching across the lady's face that this lady was a card-carrying member of the "I'd like to speak to a manager" club. It was just an expression, she'd never actually seen anyone pull a card out before, but if there was one in existence she was about to see it firsthand.

Matt finally walked around the corner after what felt like ages, but in actuality was about three minutes. "How may I help you Ma'am?"

Lucy could swear she saw smoke coming out of the lady's ears after hearing the word Ma'am. From the look on her face which was now as red as a lobster this lady's anger level had definitely increased. It was as if he had walked up and said,

"How may I help you lady who was alive while dinosaurs were still roaming the earth?".

To neither of their surprise the lady shrieked in anger which sending spittle flying everywhere. "How dare you address me as Ma'am! I have never felt so disrespected in my entire 34 years of existence!"

In Matt's defense the lady's gaudy makeup in combination with her haircut that looked like a 70s era sitcom mom's hair wasn't doing her any favors. There was also the possibility that Matt had simply thought calling her Ma'am instead of Mrs. seemed more professional.

Either way Lucy was struggling not to laugh out loud at the latest outburst. "Well, I had wanted to speak to the person in charge to find out precisely who told this incompetent buffoon to price toothbrushes like they are made out of 24 carat gold, but I see where she learned the incompetence from."

This situation was about to implode. Little did this lady know that Matt wasn't a pushover. He loathed customers who disrespected his employees and to add insult to injury she had just disrespected him. "While I suspect this exact routine has worked on other people before, you'll be sadly disappointed to find it's not going to work on me. I do not appreciate the abhorrent way you spoke of my employee and additionally me as well."

There were several gasps followed by the sound of heels stomping in place. "Young man, I demand that you call the owner of this place right now. I'm sure they will be appalled to hear about how their manager speaks to paying clientele. I'll have both of your jobs before the day is through."

Lucy wondered how Matt was going to deal with this threat because he was the owner. Was he going to tell her straight out that he was the owner, or was he going to have a little bit of fun with it?

The answer was obvious when Matt turned back to look at her with a devilish grin on his face. "Ms. Lofthouse, will you please give this guest the owner's personal number so she can express her displeasure with how she feels I have mishandled this situation?" Never in her years of working there had any customer thrown such a fit that he had to tell her to give them his personal number which she guessed was just his office number.

All the employees were aware that he had another phone that was for strictly for personal use. However, as their boss he only used his business phone when communicating with employees.

"Yes, Mr. Campbell I will do that right away." After rattling off the actual number, not the extension that was written on the gift shop's phone directory list she waited to see what would happen.

The look of utter confusion and horror as the lady heard Matt's phone start ringing was priceless. You could've heard a pin drop as Matt answered and smoothly replied, "Hello, this is Mr. Campbell speaking how can I help you?"

Lucy lost count of how many different expletives flew out of this lady's mouth after he answered.

After the lady finally gathered enough composure to venomously spew out, "I am never coming back to this overpriced hovel again. I have no clue how a man child such as yourself has good enough credit to get a bank loan to buy this place, but I hope it closes down and you are forced to declare bankruptcy."

Lucy could tell the lady thought this was a serious burn, but it wasn't if anything it just pissed Matt off more. "First of all, Ma'am, I don't owe you an explanation of how I'm able to afford anything that I purchase, and second of all I am issuing a lifetime ban effective immediately on you so you won't have to worry about choosing not to come back."

The lady opened her mouth to make a snarky response, but decided against it when he threated to call the police to escort her out of the building. Ten minutes later both her and all of her belongings were out of their lives for good. The icing on the cake was that there was a 24-hour cancelation policy and since she had already checked in the lady couldn't even get her money back. Lucy was glad that Matt was willing to stick up for his employees instead of most places that would allow clientele to speak to employees however they wanted because the almighty dollar was too good to pass up. She thanked him and then he headed back to his office to do whatever important tasks bosses usually do.

Chapter Five: Jaden and The Gift Shop Grind

She looked at the clock on her computer and almost an hour had flown by. Jaden was going to be here soon, and he was going to love hearing this story when he arrived.

Word apparently traveled fast because the first thing he said when he arrived was "So Lucy Ann, I hear you've been upsetting customers. After yesterday's tardiness you've really started trying for that worst employee of the month award."

Jaden was the only person who was allowed to use her middle name, and he knew this.

"Take that back Jaden Alexander. Yep, that's right I can play the middle name game too." She laughed as he called for a truce which she knew he would do. Both of them only used each other's middle names when they were joking around.

"So, what was the name of the lucky fellow that made Ms. Always On Time late for work?" As her bestie, he was also the only person that was allowed to make jokes about her lack of experience because he didn't actually care that she hadn't done the deed yet.

Until recently he hadn't either, but according to his own admission it had just felt like the right time. He wasn't particularly bothered by the fact that he hadn't really spoken to the guy since, but that was by his choice. When they had first met, he hadn't omitted the fact that he was inexperienced, but he had also been straight forward about the fact that he wasn't looking for something super serious at the moment. Even though they were best friends he hadn't went into further detail about the specifics and there wasn't really a need to because in their friendship both of them understood some things were meant to remain private business between the involved parties.

"I know this will be sad news, but nothing nearly as exciting as what you mentioned led to my tardiness. The power went out and I forgot to plug my phone in and set the alarms to boot." Just to add fuel to this fire she decided to cryptically follow this up with," I did have a dream about a guy this morning although I couldn't see what he looked like." She could see the wheels in his mind turning trying to figure out what that meant.

"Well, that's kinky. I'd assume that's an advanced move for a beginner though." Before he could say anything else about this dream dude or her "advanced skills" she burst into laughter.

"Get your mind out of the gutter, I meant I literally couldn't see what he looked like because his face was obstructed by the shadows."

Oh, great now it was going to sound like she was talking about Slimder Guy which was a character from a video game inspired by an urban legend that all the teens were obsessed with. She'd never played the game before, but from the description it was about a scary shadow guy that hid amongst the trees and other creepy places and dropped notes with clues. The goal was for the person playing to find all of these notes and survive until daylight without Slimder Guy jumping out and killing them. The name alone sounded too stupid for her to be interested in playing.

Now that Jaden knew she wasn't getting laid in her dreams either, she was curious what he thought her dream about this mysterious guy meant. "Maybe you're supposed to meet a guy who is tall dark and handsome or it's an indication that you'll need to look beyond the surface and into his soul to figure out if he's the right guy for you." The conversation ended there because a group of customers was near the podium waiting to be seated.

Jaden was the only server from noon until 3pm because there wasn't normally a huge rush until dinnertime. If he got really busy on weekends there was always Sarah in the bar area who could come out and help if there were no customers. If Sarah was busy too Lucy could always help get drink orders as long as no one was in the gift shop. Since the restaurant was closed after breakfast ended until noon there was no need for her to stand at the podium hosting. Sarah would help the bussers with their various cleaning duties and then bartend from noon until her shift ended at 4PM.

At 3pm one or both of the other nighttime servers would arrive depending on how many people were staying overnight.

If it was less than 300 only Cara or Wes would come in because two servers and a bartender could handle things. If there was more than that three servers and a bartender were deemed necessary. Diego was the night-time bartender who usually replaced Sarah at 4pm. Since her shift ended at 3pm she didn't know Diego that well, but Jaden said he was a nice guy.

While she was cleaning the counter a family walked into the shop. So far, they all seemed nice. There was a kid around 6 or 7, a toddler, a man and woman.

The man asked, "excuse me could you please tell me where the magnets are located." Ah, people with manners. A customer service person's favorite type of customer.

"Yes Sir, they are right there on the left side of the shop on the white rotating display." The man said thanks and went to go check.

The mom was on the opposite side of the shop helping the little ones pick out a toy. It looked like the kid was interested in one of those cars that flip when they run into the wall, and the toddler was focused on the plushies.

Lucy was trying not to seem overtly watchful. No way did she want a repeat of the customer last week who had accused her of being racist because she was "watching her too closely." In actuality the shop had just opened up and she was putting things that had fallen off a display back where they belonged. A week later she was still confused by the interaction. She hadn't even been paying attention to the woman in any way that could've been interpreted as watchful.

The woman and children moved onto the candy display and the mom picked out a pack of Gummi Dinos for them to share. When they set their items on the counter she asked, "did you find everything alright today?" The man laughed and replied "more than we needed, but yes we did." She put the car, a palm tree shaped magnet with the logo on it, the Gummi Dinos, and a plush frog into the bag and set it on the counter. The man paid with a credit card. As they were leaving, she told them "Have a nice day," and this time she meant it. When she had told the lady earlier to have a nice day it was strictly because she was being professional.

"You too, and don't work too hard," the guy said.

"Don't mind him dear, he enjoys making dad jokes. This lady is trying to work, leave her be" the woman playfully told her husband.

For every terrible customer that came through there were at least five others that were nice as could be. Most of the time people just wanted to get whatever items they came in for and go about their day. Since there were no guests in the shop she decided to put in her lunch order. A buffalo fried chicken wrap and loaded fries had been on her mind for a few hours now and her stomach was starting to make a growling sound. She could probably ask Jaden to watch her register for fifteen minutes once her food got done as long as his table had their food. It wasn't required to clock out if an employee was taking a fifteen-minute break, and the only ones required by law to take a half hour were the teenagers. The servers usually took a thirty-minute break as well, but there was always another person on the floor so it was no big deal.

She could sit in the employee break room and eat, or in the bar as long as there weren't any customers and she didn't go behind the black lines near the countertop. Her 21st birthday was in a few days, but until then she had to follow the rules and you had to be 21 to go behind the black lines. ID was required to be shown by everybody as proof of age so that the bartenders wouldn't get in trouble. Jaden had turned 21 a few weeks, but he hadn't been to any bars or the casino yet. He was waiting to experience his first time going to any 21 and over places until her birthday so they could celebrate the important milestone together.

Ding! Ding! She heard the sound of a small bell being rung. The noise was coming from the kitchen. Jaden's table had already gotten their food a minute ago so the ding meant her food was ready. She was happy to see that her favorite cook Jesse was the one who had made her food. He was an older guy in either his late 30s or early 40s. Although he didn't have a formal training, he took great pride in all the food he cooked.

Sadly, there was a misconception amongst some of society that people who hadn't gone to culinary school weren't good at cooking. A cook was typically seen as a person who merely follows recipes while chefs are generally seen as an innovative person with an eye for detail and creating new recipes. Customers rarely sent food back to the kitchen when he was there. On the other hand, there was a different cook named Shawn was a self-proclaimed chef who was an egotistical maniac whose burgers were described by employees and customers alike as being hard as hockey pucks. Then there was Marlon who was super chill and originally from Jamaica. Sometimes he would bring in traditional foods like Jerk Chicken, Fried Plantains, and banana bread for the employees to try.

There was still no one in the bar at the moment so she decided to eat in there. The first bite of her buffalo wrap was heavenly, and the fries had just the right amount of salt. She took turns dipping the fries into ketchup and the side of buffalo sauce that Jesse had put in a small plastic condiment container for her. Fifteen minutes later her belly was full, and she was ready to get back to work.

She thanked Jaden for watching her register and looked around to see if anything needed to be reorganized. There were a few price tags that had fallen off onto the floor which she could easily sweep up, but other than that there wasn't much cleaning left for her to do. After that the last daily task to check off was mopping and that wouldn't take very long. She grabbed the four wet floor signs out of the storage closet beside the cooler and placed two of them in the back corner of the shop and the other two in the entrance ways where they could easily be seen because a wet floor could be very slippery and dangerous. She also couldn't afford the costly lawsuit if a customer were to slip and fall. Two minutes later the mop bucket was set up and ready to go. The mop solution smelled like a fresh meadow or so the label on the bottle said. Whatever the smell was it was strong but amazing and the shop always smelled clean for an hour or two afterwards. Luckily the floor was dry by the time that Jaden's table came up to pay their bill.

As soon as they left the shop a few people walked in and started looking around. One of the guests purchased two drinks and a t shirt. Another bought a magnet that looked like a flip flop and some Twizzlets which were a mini strawberry shaped licorice candy. Jaden had two more tables during this time, but one was only a group of two and the other was a group of four, so he was still handling things by himself just fine. She could also hear the blender whirring so there must be a few people in the bar. A few minutes later she saw two people walking out of the bar happily sipping on frozen drinks that one of them said was a strawberry margarita. Another guest walked out with two bottles of beer in hand.

Chapter Six: Dreaming at the Stake

She looked at the clock again and it was 2pm. Only an hour left until she could go home and read one of the books, she had checked out at the library the other day. The school library doubled as the public library. It was small, but they carried her favorite book series which was a supernatural love story about a 17-year-old girl named Haley and her two best friends whose lives were changed forever when she fell in love with the new foreign exchange student who was secretly a warlock. He wasn't just any warlock either, as it turns out he was the teenage son of the warlock clan in his home country of Denmark. As if that wasn't life changing enough, she also found out that the father she had never met was also a warlock and she was a witch.

However, last week she had discovered a new series by a self-published author. So far there were only two books, but their covers looked enticing and the premise sounded good. The first book was called The Killer Hunters: Lexi and it introduced readers to two childhood best friends named Crimson and Lance who went around hunting down slashers from horror movies that were brought to life along with other supernatural baddies that were wreaking havoc on the human world. Of course, she also enjoyed reading classic books like The Grand Gratsby, To Kill A Bluejay, Bridge to Teripathia, The Crystal Menagerie, Romero and Julianne, and Of Muskrats and Men. Before she knew it Molly was there to relieve her for the day. After telling Jaden goodbye she grabbed her purse from her locker and quickly exited the building.

When she arrived home, she fixed a quick meal, took a shower, changed into pajamas, and relaxed in bed with the first Killer Hunters book. She was breathing heavily, the leaves crunching beneath her feet as the cool crisp air enveloped her.

The only warmth to be felt was the heat from the torches in the hands of the townsfolk chasing her. Her unprotected feet were starting to bleed as she ran through the forest stepping on sharp rocks and tree branches along the way. Her thin white nightgown provided little relief from the cold air and was torn in several places from getting snagged on tree branches.

She was still groggy from being startled awake by the sound of fists pounding against her front door accompanied by chants of "get the witch." She regretted not having time to think about putting on shoes as she had climbed out her bedroom window and ran towards the forest. It was easy enough to get lost during the day, but the nighttime was proving to be even worse. The moon was but a sliver in the sky, and the tall trees were obscuring any useful amount of light from coming through. She was growing tired, but she couldn't risk stopping.

She knew that the townsfolk would have no qualms about burning her at the stake if they captured her. Just this week three women had already perished after being deemed guilty of witchcraft. Trials, if the term was applicable were held, but only so that people could sleep easier at night. Pretending that the accused were getting fair treatment was instrumental in convincing themselves that they were stopping the work of the devil.

One lady had been deemed guilty because she was caught "dancing" but according to her she was merely trying to swat away a bee. Another had gotten into a quarrel with a neighbor whose cow had died a few nights later. She wasn't even sure what the last woman had been found guilty of, but innocence wasn't of high importance to people suffering from mass paranoia. Her face had multiple scratches and she could feel the blood trickling down her cheeks. Her chest was heaving, every breath more painful than the last. An owl hooted eerily amongst the trees, and she didn't even want to think about the various spiders or snakes that could be waiting to attack her.

She could hear the sound of rushing water in the distance, but she was unsure which direction it was coming from. She didn't notice the ground becoming uneven until it was too late. Suddenly she was tumbling down the side of a small downward incline. Her body was picking up speed and when she finally stopped her vision blurred and her head felt like it was it was on fire. As she drifted out of consciousness her head uncomfortably rested atop the large cold rock her head had made contact with.

Her eyes slowly fluttered open, her head still felt tender. As she tried to reach upwards to access the damage, she was horrified to realize that her hands were bound tightly with rope. She had been captured and thrown into a damp cell. How long had she been unconscious? Not that the length of time mattered in the slightest. Whatever day or night it was her trial would be held as soon as possible to rid the village of the devils supposed influence. Either way someone would come to collect her, and then she would have to plead her case before the town leader. He was a cold unnerving man with beady little eyes and a lust for power. There was no point in trying to rationalize with him. She would simply walk in state her innocence and await her cruel fate.

She was unsure of how much time had passed when the man came to collect her. As expected, she was found guilty and set to be burned at the stake later that night. Her hands and feet were bound to the large wooden pole in the center of the woodpile. Everyone in town was seemingly there and eager to see her burn as they were with the prior victims.

The town leader and his righthand men were standing in front of her with their torches lit and ready to light up the wood beneath her feet. The smell of accelerant was permeating in the air.

Chants of "Burn the Witch" were becoming louder until the town leader ordered everyone to quiet down so that he could ask the witch for her last words. "Do you wish to repent for your bodily transgressions so that your soul may be at rest after purification by fire?"

She had nothing to atone for and she would not give him the satisfaction of even speaking lest he believe she did. She shook her head no. She scanned the crowd one last time looking for even one face amongst the crowd with a sorrowful expression.

Amongst the shadows standing away from everyone else in the crowd she saw what looked like a tall man. Maybe he was standing so far away from the others because he was remorseful, and that gave her comfort as she felt the heat from the flames rising up. The pungent smell of burning flesh was in the air. The smoke filling her lungs was suffocating her and then her body started to go into shock from the pain. Screams filled the air.

Lucy abruptly woke drenched in sweat. Her sheets were soaked. That was what she got for dozing off right after reading the chapter about Scarecrow Brady. No more reading The Killer Hunters before bed for her. She looked over at her alarm clock. It was 4:45AM. She'd have to be up soon anyways and she needed to take a shower before work. No way was she showing up smelling like sweat. She had a waterproof mattress protector under her sheets so at least her mattress wouldn't stink like sweat. She pulled the sheets, covers, and pillowcases off the bed and threw them into the hamper. She could wash them after work. She had a washer and dryer in her apartment which she'd use for the pillowcases and sheets. All of the units in her building had a washer and dryer provided for $25 extra dollars a month.

There was a public laundromat located in the center of the apartment complex, so that people could wash their items if they chose not to pay the extra $25 but anyone in the apartments could use it. It was worth paying $3.50 to wash and dry the comforter in one of the industrial size washer and dryers to save time and make sure it dried properly. There was also the benefit of not putting additional strain on the washer and dryer in her apartment. Every week she would wash her sheets and pillowcases on Monday night, but it was Sunday morning so only a day earlier than usual. Her comforter on the other hand was washed on a biweekly schedule on Monday night. Fortunately, one extra wash wasn't going to break the bank. After that she took a quick shower, had a light breakfast, and got dressed for work.

Chapter Seven:

Gambling on a Birthday

Lucy was standing in front of her full-length mirror looking at her outfit which was an amethyst purple v neck dress with small silver rhinestones accents that was just above knee length. It wasn't her usual style of dress, but Jaden had insisted that she wear something stunning to the casino. She did have to admit it accented her curves well. At least that made up for having to travel an hour and a half to the nearest mall to find it. Plus, it was on sale for $50. It was a nice dress, but no way would she have paid $150 for it.

The shoe store at the mall was having a summer sale so she was able to find a nice pair of 3-inch black heels with silver straps for $30. Again, not her typical style but according to Jaden and the sales clerk they went well with her new dress. She had put both items on her credit card which had a $1000 limit and she barely used it so she could afford to splurge just a little.

It was a special occasion after all. As of today, May 22 she was finally 21 years old. Her hair was pulled back into an updo described as a fancy messy bun updo with three tendrils (loose curls) she had followed from an internet video. With Jaden's help her hair had been secured by approximately one hundred bobby pins. In the front there were two accent curls on either side of her face. The shade of eyeshadow on her lids were close to the same shade as her dress with a lighter purple shade on the inner corner, gold on the crease, and finally a light cream color just above the crease. She went with black mascara and a silver winged eye liner, which she had used a tool to help achieve because no way would she have been able to do that freehanded. For her lips she had used one of those Ph reacting glosses which was supposed to be personalized to suit the users perfect shade of pink. It had taken her an hour and a half to achieve this look which had gotten Jaden's seal of approval judging by the fact he referred to it as "smokin'".

Jaden was wearing a lightweight baby blue short-sleeve polo shirt, black khaki pants, and dress shoes. She wasn't sure what specific word to use for Jaden's outfit, but it suited him nicely. Especially the shirt that brought out his dark bluish green eyes.

Before they left, they did a double check to make sure that they had IDs, money, and cellphones. Lucy had placed all of her important items in a silver clutch she had bought at the mall a few years ago. They were both off tomorrow and had split the cost of the cheapest hotel room with two beds at the casino so there was no worry of either of them driving home while under the influence. They were taking Jaden's car which was a Grey 2009 Hondera Civic. Their overnight bags were already in the car and had been checked to ensure all necessary items were accounted for. The Casino wasn't a far drive, but it was in the next town over which was named Moon Hollow. Yeah, the city names were pretty weird around here.

Thirty minutes later they pulled into the parking lot of Eternal Night Resort and Casino. Driving by it she had never realized how large this place was. They grabbed their bags and headed inside to check in. As they stepped near the door they were greeted by a muscular man in a suit wearing a name tag that said Alejandro.

"Good evening patrons and welcome to Eternal Night, Moon Hollow's most luxurious hotel and casino. May I show you to the front desk to check in or are you here for casino only?"

They both answered "checking in" at the same time which was followed by laughter.

Alejandro replied "Wonderful, please follow me and our helpful receptionist, Tessa will get you checked in."

As they neared the reception desk Alejandro said hello to a blonde woman who looked to be in her mid-20s.

She greeted them with a smile. "Hello and welcome to our establishment. My name is Tessa; how may I assist you lovely folks tonight?" The customer service skills were top notch here.

Lucy responded, "Hello Tessa, we would like to get checked in please and thank you." It was very important for Lucy to always use manners when speaking to fellow customer service personnel. She knew firsthand how rude some people could be and she never wanted anyone to perceive her that way.

"First I will need to know the last name the room was reserved under, I will also need a credit card for any incidentals. For now, only a $1 hold will be placed on the card which will be reversed after you check out if no incidentals occur." Tessa politely stated.

The room was reserved under Jaden's name so he answered, "The last name is Evans and here is my credit card."

After typing some information into the computer Tessa handed them a pamphlet with their room keys and the room number written inside. Jaden thanked Tessa and took a quick glance. Then he handed it to Lucy so she could look at it. They would be staying in Room 303, which would be very easy for both of them to remember because there was a band with the same name but spelled different.

"There are three sets of elevators, and the closest ones are right over there. When you get in just hold your room key over the scanner, and it will turn green then push the button for the floor you are staying on. Once again thank you for staying at this hotel and may both of you have an excellent stay." Both of them thanked her for her time and assistance, then it was off to the elevators.

Jaden pushed the circular Call Button on the elevator that was located on the righthand side which from the Hall Lantern indicated that the elevator was traveling down from the fifth floor. As they waited the hallway was so quiet that they could hear the whirring sound of the elevator cables descending from above. The brakes made a small squeak as it came to a stop on the first floor. When the door opened two elderly couples, and two people who looked to be mid 20s early 30s stepped out. All of them were dressed in expensive looking formal wear. The women were all wearing diamond earrings and necklaces. Everything about their attire screamed that these people had the type of money that they weren't concerned about winning or losing at the casino.

Jaden and Lucy stepped off to the side to allow everyone enough room to pass. "Excuse me dearie," one of the elderly ladies said as she slowly shuffled around Lucy and into the hallway. The woman's husband was not as nice. As he was passing by, he gave a disapproving look at Lucy and Jaden's attire. As he did this, she noticed that he was wearing an expensive looking watch on his left hand. The type that probably cost at least two times both hers and Jaden's combined yearly salary.

In the elevator Jaden scanned his room key and pushed the button for floor 3. As the elevator started moving, she found herself lost in thought. What did this seemingly nice woman see in him? Other than the obvious answer which was money, and he clearly had plenty of it. Maybe she had married him long ago when women were housewives waiting for their men to return from active duty. While it was indicative of the times of old, Lucy was glad that in current society women could choose to have a career or be a housewife.

Though the idea of falling in love and spending a lifetime with the man she loved sounded nice, there was one thing she knew for sure. Motherhood was not for her. No, she didn't despise children or look down on others for wanting to have children, it was just a lot of responsibility. According to Diane it was also very costly having to pay for essentials like formula, diapers, wipes, clothes, and babysitters. There were also other key factors like the abysmal state of healthcare and the complications that could arise during a pregnancy. She heard the elevator ding, and it snapped her back to reality. They were here to celebrate a one in a lifetime milestone for both of them. It was time to have fun; not worry about the disapproving stare of a rich old dude she'd never see again after tonight.

When the elevator doors opened, they looked for the hallway sign to see which direction they needed to go to find their room. The sign was easy to spot and indicated that rooms 300-315 were on the left. When they got to the room, she entered her room key into the keycard reader which flashed green for a second then made a low chiming noise to indicate the door was open. She felt against the wall for the light switch and waited for the lights to come on before stepping in. She half expected to see Scarecrow Brady lying in wait on the bed. Man, that book had made an impression on her.

The walls were a rich cream color accented by touches of light gray. The lighting was soft, but warm. In the corner of the room there was an elegant light grey velvet armchair. The desk and matching chair looked high end. There was a 40" flat screen tv atop the TV cabinet. There was a nightstand on the side of each bed with a small wall lamp above. There were two landscape watercolor paintings above the two queen beds. Beds which looked comfortable, and the comforters were wrinkle free. Hopefully the housekeepers here were getting paid exceptionally well.

This room was stunning. The bathroom had a large tub/ shower combo with a waterfall shower head and frosted glass doors. The countertop for the sink was made of grey granite and the mirror above the sink was a frameless anti-fog LED style. This hotel was pulling out all the stops to make sure guests understood why it was an award-winning luxury hotel. They set their overnight bags in the wardrobe that was located by the door.

Now that they were all settled in it was time to go find the casino entrance. Lucy grabbed her purse which she had set on the desk and made sure she had put her room key card somewhere she could easily find it later. Two small spritzes of perfume later and one last check in the mirror and she was ready to go. She always kept a mini perfume bottle of Fascination by Bridgette Stakes in her purse. Bridgette Stakes was the world-famous Princess of Pop, but she had taken a break from music and founded a line of super popular perfumes. Jaden didn't have to bother putting on any more cologne. It was a running joke that one teensy spray of men's cologne could last a lifetime.

After checking to make sure the door was completely closed, they headed back towards the elevators. Lucy pushed the down button on the wall and looked at the Hallway Lanterns which said that the elevators were on the sixth and eighth floor respectively. Two minutes later the elevator on the left-hand side opened up.

There were two women and a man already inside so Lucy and Jaden went to the opposite corner of where the three were standing together.

"First floor please and thank you," Lucy said to the woman standing closest to the elevator buttons.

"You're welcome," the woman responded.

Then the three went back to quietly discussing whatever they had been talking about prior to the elevator stopping for Jaden and Lucy. When they got off the elevator, they looked for the sign in the hallway that would indicate which way the entrance to the casino was. Apparently, it was down the hall and to the right. The three other people in the elevator were also headed to the Casino so they followed them.

As they approached the glass doors there was man wearing a shirt that said "Security" with a name tag that said "Mike" standing in front of the door.

"I will need to see everyone's licenses to enter, please have them out and ready for me to check." Mike asked the line.

When it was her turn to show Mike her license, he looked at it very carefully. Her license was still vertical which was an easy way to spot if the person was under 21. There were exceptions of course for instance it being her 21st birthday and people who were over 21 but waiting until their next license renewal. In general, though, everyone over 21 had a horizontal license or switched to it as soon as possible to avoid confusion.

Since Jaden had turned 21 a few weeks ago his was horizontal now, and the security guard had checked his in 5 seconds flat. After studying hers for what felt like hours but was in actuality probably 2 minutes tops, he handed her back her license.

He chuckled and said, "Freshly 21. I remember that year. Some of it anyways. Lots and lots of alcohol involved. Both of you can go in, have fun and win big tonight." That last part was probably something his job was mandated to say because it was no secret that the motto of gambling was "The House Always Wins."

They had no sooner stepped foot into the casino when another security guard, whose name tag said Barry approached and said, "Both of you stop right there, I need to have a talk with you."

That didn't quite seem normal, but they weren't going to risk getting thrown in casino jail or worse real jail for disobeying orders.

He must have sensed that they were worried because he quickly followed it up with, "Sorry I didn't mean to worry either of you. Miss, you were the 100,000th person to come through the casino. You have won a voucher for $25 and a free drink of your choosing."

Well, that was unexpected, but it was definitely better than the scenarios that had been flashing through her mind.

"Next time dude just lead with that last part please," Jaden said.

Barry started to apologize again, "I hope your experience hasn't been ruined in any way."

Barry's phone started ringing and then he stepped away for a moment. The only thing they could hear from where they were standing was "Yes Sir, I will inform them." He was on the phone for about another minute then he walked back over to them. "The owner wishes to personally hand you the voucher and congratulate you on being the 100,000th patron of this establishment. I will wait here with you until he arrives and then I must get back to the security office."

Being up $25 before they had even hit the slots was pretty amazing. She was glad that balloons and confetti hadn't been released from the ceiling while a surprise camera crew jumped out and surrounded her asking how it felt to be the 100,000th person to visit the casino. That would have been absolutely mortifying. She hated the thought of hundreds of eyes focusing solely on her. She wondered what this mystery owner was going to look like. She'd known plenty of people who had been to this casino and not a single one of them had ever mentioned seeing the owner.

Chapter Eight: First Encounter

Speaking of eyes on her she started to feel like someone was watching her. She became suddenly aware that a guy wearing a black luxury suit with a dark blue v neck shirt underneath was headed in their direction. His eyes seemed to be focused on her as if they were the only two people in the room. Was he actually walking in slow motion or was she imagining things? He was incredibly tall. If her estimation was correct, he had to be around 6 ft 4. Maybe taller. Dark blonde hair that was parted to one side. His eyes were a cool, medium dark blue and reminded her of beautiful waves rolling across the ocean. Or maybe it was the sea, either way she was lost in them.

She could only hope that she looked more composed than she felt. If her tongue was hanging out, she was never going to hear the end of it from Jaden. He would write it in her eulogy and read it out loud at her funeral. He wasn't the type Jaden normally went for, but she couldn't blame him if he was thinking the same things as her about this particular guy. This man was almost unnaturally handsome. He was standing right beside Barry now. He whispered something into Barry's ear, and then he left leaving just the three of them standing there.

His eyes were still focused on her. It truly felt like he was staring into her soul. Butterflies were fluttering in her stomach. She could see his lips start to move, but the sound of her own heartbeat was drowning out every other sound in existence. Jaden tapped her on the shoulder. Oh shit, he probably thought she was having a medical emergency or something. She turned to look at him and he was mouthing "are you okay?". She nodded yes, because at this moment she wasn't sure she was capable of forming a coherent sentence.

She saw the man start to extend his hand toward her, so she extended hers to meet his and started to shake it. Was her palm sweaty? The last thing she needed was for this man's hand to be covered in her sweat. No, it must be fine. He hadn't recoiled in disgust. This time when he started to speak, she actually heard what he was saying. He had an accent. Just when she thought he couldn't get any hotter he had to go and have an accent. She wasn't sure where he was from, but it was for sure nowhere near Shadow Ridge or Moon Hollow.

"I am the owner of this establishment, Noah Eastman, may I ask what your name is Miss?" Noah said in a smooth and velvety voice.

Why was she suddenly drawing a blank on her own name? In 21 years, she had never forgotten her own name. Why, was her mind so scattered by this man's presence? Finally, after what felt like ages she managed to remember it. " My name is Lucy Lofthouse."

He pulled a piece of paper from inside his jacket pocket and handed it to her. "Here is your $25 voucher. It has been a pleasure to meet you, Miss Lofthouse. May I interest you in a VIP Tour?"

Let me guess there's going to be a quick stop by his bedroom on this 'VIP Tour' she muttered under her breath and giggled. There was a glimmer of mischief in his eyes as a playful smile started to form.

He started to speak in that smooth and velvety voice and said "Well, I hadn't planned on showing you my bedroom, but if you insist, I am happy to oblige a request from such a pretty woman. However, fair warning it would not be a quick stop." He winked and flashed a charming smile as he finished the sentence.

The wind felt like it had been knocked out of her. How the absolute hell had he heard what she said? Jaden doubled over in laughter. In a way she couldn't blame him for having that reaction, but she definitely going to get him back for it later. Right now, she was more concerned with the fact that she had practically invited herself into this man's bedroom, and he was more than happy to accept the invitation. Her cheeks felt flushed; they were probably as red as an apple. If she was a snake she would've already slithered into the nearest hiding place.

Jaden who hadn't spoken a single word up to this point but had no trouble laughing decided to respond. "Mr. Eastman, what my friend meant to say was that we would enjoy a VIP Tour." Oh, so now he could talk. She shot him a look that could've killed him on the spot.

Mr. Eastman gestured for them to follow him. As they started to walk wherever he was taking them he turned back and spoke to Lucy directly. "I can tell that I have embarrassed you with my response to what was clearly something I was not meant to hear, and was said in jest."

He was leading them towards the bar. Oh yeah, she had won a free drink. She had no clue what she was going to order. She searched her mind trying to remember anything she had heard people ordering from the bar at work. Once again, her mind was blank. Luckily there was menu on the bar when they approached it.

First, they handed their IDs to the bartender whose name was Adeline, and then Jaden ordered a Long Island Iced Tea. She looked for something that sounded like it contained more juice than alcohol. She ordered something called a Malibu Sunset which had a coconut flavored rum, pineapple, orange juice, and Grenadine. It was garnished with an orange slice and two cherries. Mr. Eastman asked for something that he called "The Bloody Eastman" which must have been some sort of off menu specialty drink bartenders kept behind the counter just for him. Maybe it was a variation of the Bloody Mary that he had named after himself. The bartender poured it from a fancy golden bottle with strange markings. There was a matching goblet that the bartender poured it into. It must have tasted amazing because he was swirling it around in one hand savoring every sip like people on television did when they were drinking 80-year-old wine from vineyards in Italy.

They stopped in front of a door with a glass window. There was a large sign above the door that said "Blood Donations".

Mr. Eastman seemed especially proud as he started to talk about this room. "Every year The Eternal Night Casino donates a large portion of our proceeds to various charitable organizations." He continued, "We are proud partners with many hospitals across the state including the county hospital here in Moon Hollow." The way he talked about it this venture implied this wasn't a simple tax write off. A wealthy casino owner who truly cared about such a cause was quite admirable.

"There are two onsite nurses for each shift so that patrons who wish to can donate blood. This helps keep hospitals in the state stocked with blood for emergency situations. It is both a rewarding experience to help people and we offer $50 cash or casino credit for a single pint of blood." As he said this a smile crept over his face.

She had never heard of a blood donation center inside a casino before. It was an odd arrangement, but if it was helping people then who was she to judge. People did like to gamble, and hospitals were always in need of blood. It was a win-win situation. Mr. Eastman informed them that there was one last stop on the tour, and then he would leave them to enjoy the rest of their night. The sign above the door said "High Rollers Room" and was separated from the rest of the machines. Every machine in the room had a $100 minimum.

They stopped in front of one and watched as a man in a business suit put an entire stack of $100s in without a second thought. He just kept pulling the lever not even paying attention to whether or not he was winning. Another lady was at a machine that had 5 dancing cats running across the screen which according to the screen above meant that she was about to start playing free games for a chance to win big. Lucy couldn't even fathom the idea of having enough money to spend all her time in here.

She and Jaden had planned on playing the penny slots. Maybe a dollar max if they were doing well on a machine. One of the machines had a flashing green light and the machine itself was making a bunch of happy sounds. Chimes and dings galore. Lucy stepped closer and saw that the woman's machine said she had just won $5,000. A security guard was standing next to the machine as an employee was doing something Mr. Eastman called 'a hand payout'. This was something that meant a casino worker would literally hand you your winnings at the machine instead of collecting your earnings at the money counter which was called "the cage".

Directly following that explanation Mr. Eastman turned to them and stated, "I must retire back to my office now. Goodnight, Miss Lofthouse."

Then he reached for her hand and as he did this, he said something in a language she didn't understand. "Tills vi ses igen, min kärlek". When he finished speaking, he kissed her hand.

Her heart started beating rapidly and she was sure her eyelids were fluttering. Internally she was felt like melting into a pile of goo. She wasn't sure how to respond back to what he said since she couldn't understand it, so she just flashed him a smile. Then he turned to Jaden and stuck out his hand.

As he was shaking his hand Mr. Eastman said, "Apologies, I didn't catch your name earlier Sir." Lucy hadn't realized that she hadn't introduced Jaden earlier. How rude of her to forget to introduce her best friend. Clearly, she was incapable of functioning properly when Mr. Eastman was around.

"It's Jaden Evans, thank you again for showing us around tonight." Well at least one of them was managing to use their manners.

Once there was enough distance between them and Mr. Eastman to ensure that he wouldn't hear them Jaden turned to Lucy. "Girl, what was that? For a second I actually thought you were going to jump that man's bones when he offered."

Lucy honestly didn't have a rational explanation for her behavior. To be honest at the moment she wasn't entirely sure she wouldn't have gladly let him rock her world. Regardless, she needed to say something. "There was something magnetic about him. I looked into his eyes, and it felt like we were two puzzle pieces perfectly designed for each other." She had never felt such an intense connection before.

Jaden always one to hype her up said, "Maybe you should go for it, the feeling seemed mutual." Lucy couldn't argue with that.

When he had kissed her hand, she could swear she saw him try to hide a sly smile afterwards. It was almost as if he sensed that he had elicited a strong reaction in her. Surely with his striking looks he could get any woman he wanted. He was clearly way above her league. It was time to focus on why they were here in the first place.

"Let's just go get another drink, turn this voucher in at the cage, and then play some slots and see how far this free $25 gets us." This time Jaden decided that both of them should order cocktails with silly names so he got one named 'Hanky Panky' and she got something called 'Fuzzy Navel". This time they told the bartender that they wanted to take the drink to go so she put it into a plastic glass.

Next, they made their way to the cage where a helpful employee named Ella helped Lucy exchange her voucher for cash. There were hundreds of machines to choose from. Each one cooler than the last. Eventually Lucy decided upon one that was based upon a popular children's film about an eccentric candy confectioner. The instructions at the top of the machine stated that this machine had digital spinning reels. This meant that pressing the button labeled spin would automatically cause the reels or lines to start spinning on screen. There were several "paylines" which were made up of various horizontal, vertical, or zig zag patterns across the screens. The more you bet the more paylines would be active.

For instance, betting .5 cents would get you one payline,.10 cents would get you two, .25 cents three .50 was five paylines and 10 of them for $1. The max bet on this machine was $5 per spin. You could also just set the amount you wanted to bet and then push a button with various line amounts up to 25 lines. That could get pretty expensive though so it was probably best they just stick to a set bet and the amount of lines that could be hit off that.

From the looks of it the first step to potentially hitting big was to have 5 chocolate bars line up on any payline at the same time. That would trigger a set amount of "free mini games" based upon the amount of additional chocolate bars in total that had appeared on the screen at the time that the free games were triggered. During the mini games if patrons were to get ten chocolate bars and the confectioner on the screen at the same time, they would win the big jackpot of $5,000. Five chocolate bars and the confectioner at the same time would get the mini jackpot of $1,000.

Matching various characters or candies in a payline would win different small amounts which were listed. At random times the screen would suddenly switch to a "wild function" which meant only five huge symbols would appear on the screen in total. If five golden eggs appeared on that screen the person playing would win $25,000. The odds of anyone hitting the last one were probably 1 in 1,000,0000. Betting .25 was probably the best way to start considering that this was free money. They took turns pushing the button that said play 3 lines and then the spin button. During one of the turns they triggered a set of mini games and after all was said and done, they had won $50. The machine was fun, but since they were still playing on free money they decided to cash out and see if they could win big on a different machine. A cash out voucher with the casino's name, validation date, a barcode, and the $50 amount automatically printed out of the machine.

It was Jaden's turn to pick out a machine, so they walked around until he found one that piqued his interest. They held the voucher over the scanner on the machine and it transferred the money as credit to the machine. This machine was fortune teller themed. If 3 crystal ball symbols and 2 psychics appeared in any payline it would trigger the minigames. If 4 crystal balls and the psychic were in the same payline it would not only trigger the minigames but would automatically win the mini jackpot of $500 in addition to whatever money accumulated during the minigames. 5 crystal balls and the big jackpot of 10,000 would hit. An image of the psychic holding the crystal ball was the scatter symbol for this game and if 3 of those appeared anywhere on the screen those would stay on the screen and then 10 free bonus spins would be awarded and if at the end of those spins the screen was showing 7 of those images the mega jackpot of 50,000 would be won. After a few spins they were down to $30. While the game looked cool the odds had not been in their favor on this game. It was once again time to cash out and find a different game to play.

The next machine they decided to play was themed around a popular fairytale about a girl and 3 bears. This one was different from the others they had previously played. The instructions at the top said it was " a progressive machine" which meant it was connected to other machines nearby. On this type of machine, the amount of the jackpot would increase in small preset increments as the number of plays on the machines increased. Once any player hit the jackpot the amount would be reset. The catch was that in order to qualify for the jackpot players had to be betting the maximum amount which for this machine was $1. After several unsuccessful attempts they decided to cashout and take their remaining $20 elsewhere.

While betting lower amounts had resulted in being able to play more, it was time to try their hand at betting big. There was a huge machine against the wall that had only 3 lines. The game was simple for $5 a spin players would pull a lever on the side. Getting 3 of the same symbols horizontally on any line indicated a win. If players got three leprechaun symbols it was an automatic $200. Three rainbow symbols and it was $500. Three cauldrons of gold and the top prize was $2,500. Four spins later and the last of the free money was gone. At least they been able to play for almost 2 hours without spending a single dime. Plus, they still had the $100 they had each brought to play with.

First it was time for one last drink. This time they both decided to get something called a Tequila Sunrise. Since they were each using their own money now, they decided to split up and see if playing different machines would yield better results. Lucy set her drink down next to a machine that was fairy themed. She put $20 into the machine, bet .25, and pushed the spin button. The first few spins were duds, but then she got 3 scatter symbols which triggered 20 free games. She pushed the button again to start them and after a few spins she won 10 more free games. By end of the free spins, she was up to $200.

The machine was making a blend of happy noises as animated coins and fireworks were playing on the screen. Luckily, she had quickly figured out how to turn the machine noises lower because when it first started someone had left it turned up so loud, she was sure people could hear it in the next county. Jaden had heard it from the machine he was at which was around 10 feet away. He knew it was her because she was the only person anxiously fiddling in her chair with crazy eyes while looking for any instructions on how to adjust the volume. He gave her a thumbs up sign. Once she had cashed out, she went to go check on how Jaden was doing. She arrived just in time to see him trigger some bonus games of his own and see him get up to $125. She wasn't sure what amount he had started with but it was at least $25 than what he'd started with. It was getting pretty late so they decided to play a few more games and then head back up to the room and get some sleep. After they turned their final vouchers in at the cages Lucy had $250, and Jaden had $200. Not bad for their first time in the casino.

It was probably birthday luck. Neither one of them planned on making a habit of coming back. Gambling was fun, but it was no secret that it could become an addictive habit.

There were commercials for a hotline to call if you need help to stop gambling that would play on tv sometimes. It was a good thing that they were off work tomorrow because they were both feeling residual effects of the alcoholic beverages they had ingested. It was very easy to see why Barry the security guy had said he didn't remember the year he turned 21. In the future they would definitely have to remember to heed the warnings of people who had warned them to pace themselves. The way people had always described hangovers didn't sound fun to either of them.

As they exited the casino, she found herself taking one last glance around the room to see if she saw Mr. Eastman. By tomorrow he would probably forget about all about her. He probably saw thousands of people come through this casino in a week's time. Maybe it was for the best that she didn't see him. Admittedly the thought that he would forget her that quickly made her sad, but she would always remember the brief but puzzling time they had spent together. When they made it back to their room after changing and getting ready for bed, they both drifted off to sleep as soon as their heads hit the pillows.

She was carefully walking down the staircase in a beautiful royal purple ball gown. Her hair was parted down the middle and the hair on the crown of her head was braided and pulled back into a bun. There were large, soft curls on the side that had been deliberately left out and smaller face framing curls at the front. When she got to the bottom of the stairs, he was waiting for her with his hand outstretched. He looked distinguished wearing a black tailcoat with a white ruffled shirt and grey trousers. The strands of his golden dark blonde hair glimmered like rays of sunlight on a hot summer day. His blue eyes were mesmerizing. It was impossible to look away, but then again, she had no desire to look away. There was a slight scruff to his usually clean-shaven face that was hiding the dimple in his chin.

He was the most captivating man she had ever laid eyes upon. She took his hand and let him lead her onto the dance floor. Their arms were intertwined as he twirled her gracefully waltzing across the floor in time with the harmonious music. When the dance ended, he bowed and then he leaned down and whispered softly near her ear. He asked her to meet him outside in the garden in five minutes. They would have to be careful to avoid anyone noticing them sneaking off. They were betrothed, but it was forbidden to engage in any unbecoming behavior such as being alone together. Such notions were not allowed until they were officially wed.

The plan was for him to leave first in search of the restroom, and she would simply be in need of fresh air which was not unusual behavior. Her corseted dress was hard to breathe in, but it was the price one had to pay to look fashionable or so the designer had stated.She often visited the garden at night unaccompanied by her guards. Once they were completely sure that they were alone he leaned down and pressed his soft lips to hers. She felt his hand move to the nape of her neck moving his thumb to gently stroke the side of her neck. He pulled her in closer and started caressing her lower back. His lips brushed against her cheeks slowly moving down to her neck planting soft kisses along the way. She bit her lip as she tried and failed to hide an involuntary whimpering noise. Her hand moved from his hips and ran her fingers along his side until her hand was gently tangled in his hair.

He made a low growl sound in approval. He paused momentarily. "You are the most strikingly beautiful woman I have ever seen. I cannot wait to get you alone and ravish you on our wedding night."

She couldn't imagine what he meant by that if what he was currently doing didn't fit his definition of ravishing. At this moment she would have settled for him loosening the ties on the back of her dress. If breathing had been hard for her before the things he had been doing moments before had left her completely breathless. Oh, to hell with it why wait until their wedding night? She was ready to let him rip this dress off her and throw her on the ground on top of the dress. They were so caught up in their passion that they hadn't noticed that they were no longer alone.

Two of her guards were staring at them. "Your parents will be most unhappy to hear about your betrothed attempting to defile you before the wedding. There was a strange ringing noise and then she woke up.

Why had she set her alarm for 8 AM? At least it hadn't woken Jaden up. There was no going back to sleep now. Parts of the dream were hazy, but she remembered being in a fancy ballgown and dancing with a man that looked like Mr. Eastman. There was no denying she was intrigued by him, but dreaming up fantasy scenarios where they were betrothed was insane. She was an average looking girl from a small town and he was a breathtakingly gorgeous casino owner. The whole chance meeting leading to instantly falling in love and having a whirlwind romance only happened in the movies. Didn't it?

Going off the deep end. Losing her mind. Down Bad. All accurate ways she would refer to her state of mind at the present moment. Three weeks had passed since her trip to the casino and thoughts of Noah Eastman were still randomly swimming through her mind. She had met him and spent time with him for an hour. How had he managed to make such a lasting impression on her? Sure, he was the most attractive man she had seen in real life, but she didn't even know him. What if he was leading a double life as The Moon Hollow Strangler? It's not as if there were news reports about people mysteriously going missing, so that was off the table. She had obviously watched one too many true crime shows. So far, the only crime the man had committed was unknowingly stealing her heart.

One day she'd open the local newspaper and his marriage announcement would be inside. Local Casino Owner, Noah Eastman marries Supermodel Stella Valentine. After the wedding she'd see him on the front page of Beautiful People Magazine with his famous new bride. Underneath in smaller print it would say "See the exclusive wedding photos here!" First, she had dreamed she was marrying him and now she was imagining marrying him off to a supermodel. What was going on with her these days? She had never even had a serious relationship and here she was thinking she had a chance with him. Maybe her hanging out with Jaden would distract her from these irrational thoughts.

Two hours later they were at her favorite restaurant, The Flaming Wok! She ordered her favorite General Tso's Shrimp Fried rice, and an eggroll. Jaden ordered his favorite Broccoli Beef and Lo Mein Noodles. The portions were decent here, so like usual they would take the rest home as leftovers. While they waited for their food to arrive, they discussed meeting later at Jaden's place to watch the newest episode of Criminal Trackers season 4 together. It was a show about a team of FBI Agents who hunted down criminals by profiling various behaviors. Since they were both off on Wednesday nights, they had standing plans to watch it. Going out to eat beforehand was optional because it was expensive, but sometimes it was nice to splurge. Jaden's apartment was just a few doors down from hers so it was convenient for both of them. They could've tried to get a two-bedroom place, but even in a friendship as strong as theirs it was nice to have alone time.

Jaden's place had the same layout as hers. A small kitchen on the lefthand side that was attached to the front room, a laundry nook in the hallway, a bathroom, and his bedroom. Currently there were both sitting on the couch which was a navy-blue traditional sofa. It had a matching recliner, both of which he'd found on sale at one of those "going out of business" sales. She didn't remember the name of the store but it had been in the mall. His coffee table was rectangular and had fabric storage containers underneath. It was from a sale on some online site. If he needed something he could always find a sale somewhere. His TV was a 50 inch that he had found on sale for $500 the day after Thanksgiving. $200 was tips he'd saved up for a few months and he put the rest on his credit card so he counted it as only paying $300 for a reputable brand that most people were paying twice that amount for.

Time To Crime (TV Show)

It was just about time for Criminal Trackers to start. The preview for this week's episode had been a doozy. Last season there had been a criminal that had gotten away and was in the wind. Since then, the guy had been sending the team photos of themselves at different crime sites, but it was always from different angles so they hadn't been able to figure out where he was hiding. He was a master at disguising himself when he committed crimes, so they weren't even sure what he looked like anymore. He had escaped by faking a medical emergency and knocking out the medics on the way to the hospital. Would this week be when he would slip up and end up behind bars again?

The episode opened up with the head of the team Elizabeth Price in her office reading a file that was labeled confidential in bold print. Another team member CJ, walked into the office and she quickly shut the file without time to see anything but the name Pete Harper and a blurry photo. It was time for everyone to meet for the briefing on this week's Criminal deviant which was an unknown person who was leaving their victims in various bodies of water across several cities to erase potential clues as to their identity or exact hunting grounds. By the end of the episode, they solved the crime and figured out that it was actually a team of two who were working together to avoid getting caught. One of the people had slipped up and accidentally ran a red light while driving to the dumpsite and a red-light camera had captured a crystal-clear image. No big surprise they squealed on their partner to try and avoid life in prison. Sadly, regarding Pete Harper the episode ended on a cliffhanger with the team still unable to find him. Additionally, another picture of the team with a photo of a new victim was left taped to Elizabeth Price's front door. Things had been made personal. How would this affect the team going forward now that not even the home of their team leader was safe?

"Guess we'll have to wait to see how things turn out on next week's episode," Jaden said with an exasperated sigh.

Lucy nodded in agreement. It was time to talk about something she'd been dying to know all night "So how's the online dating thing going?"

Last week Jaden had created a profile on some new website that advertised 75% of users met their current partner in 6 months or less.

"I talked to one or two guys, but both of them lived an hour away, and I'm not looking for anything long distance." Jaden said with a shrug.

She hoped he'd find a good guy somewhere close because if anyone deserved to find happiness it was him. She decided to change the subject before he could ask her anything about the subject she wished to avoid at the moment. Her love life or lack thereof. "Let's make some popcorn and find a movie to watch."

Jaden had a pretty decent collection of movies as did she so it was always easy to find something to watch.

"Oh, I'll make the popcorn if you find the movie, but I know why you're changing the subject Lucy Ann."

He knew her so well. Sometimes that was the only bad thing about having a best friend for so long. It felt like he could read her mind, and right now hers was kind of a mess.

"Jaden Alexander, sometimes I think you should start paying me rent with the amount of time you spend poking around in my head rent free."

He playfully hit her shoulder in response to the comment so she did the same thing back to him. It only took Lucy a moment to find the movie she was looking for. "Do you want to watch Stupidocracy?"

They had watched it dozens of times but it never got old.

"Sounds good to me," Jaden called back from the kitchen.

When the popcorn was done Jaden brought the two bowls into the front room and sat on the couch handing one of the bowls to her. Once they had each added enough salt for their liking it was time to start the movie.

The premise of the movie was that two people of opposite genders and average intelligence signed up for a top-secret government sleep study experiment that ended up going awry. After they were placed in indestructible pods, what started as a yearlong study turned into two hundred years after the Area 41 military base they are on was accidentally destroyed during an earthquake. When the pair wakes up after their slumber is disturbed by a landfill avalanche in 2205, society is much different and dumber than it was when they were placed in hibernation mode.

Due to the dislike of government and subsequent societal collapse there was a steep decline of well-educated people having children while there was a sharp incline in the amount of the dumbest people in society reproducing like bunny rabbits. As a result of this, the two main characters were now the two smartest people in society. Crops had been nearly obliterated because they were being watered with Berry Blast Flavorade instead of water.

The most popular television show was called Bonked! which was a show filled with clips of people being hit in the noggin with strange items like rubber chickens and breakaway chairs.

After being placed in a correctional facility for the crime of their pods crashing into a local person's home one of them manages to escape by tricking a guard and is then employed by the governor to fix the towns crop issues within the week or be sent back to prison. Along the way there is mention of a time travel machine that can take them back to 2005 and fix things, but it turns out that the time machine is actually a forgotten theme park ride. Since traveling back to their original timeline is a bust the two decide to try and improve the current society.

After successfully fixing the local crop issues and other things that improve their city word spreads around the nation resulting in the two being declared President and First Lady. Left with the choice to allow society to keep becoming dumber or procreate and hope that their children and subsequent descendants would rebalance the intelligence scales they decide to get married and have 3 children hoping for the best. By the time the movie ended it was getting pretty late and Lucy was getting tired, but her apartment was only a two-minute walk so Jaden walked her to her door and they said their goodnights. After taking a very quick shower and completing her usual bedtime routine she was finally ready for bed.

Chapter Nine: To Sea or Not to Sea

Waves were crashing back and forth against the side of the boat. The crisp sea air was burning her nostrils filling them from the overwhelming amount of salt in the air. The latest wave of nausea was wreaking havoc on her body. Food sources were getting scarce. Not that eating was an appetizing thought at the moment as a result of the unexpected seasickness she was plagued with. Hopefully things would be alright once they arrived to the new world. Traveling through the winter had proven to be harsh. Most of the passengers had perished and many more would surely perish upon their arrival. Tensions were growing higher as the journey became more perilous. Hunger had a way of driving some people mad. Unfortunately, the sea and illness had not been the only thing that claimed lives aboard the ship. Some of the remaining passengers had already resorted to doing the unthinkable in order to survive and preserve rations. It was best not to think of these things. As bleak as things were looking, she was comforted by the fact that she still had him. She could feel herself growing weaker by the day, but the thought of starting a new life with him in the promised land was what kept her going. The Mayflower had almost sunk twice already during the journey due to the unpredictability of the stormy seas. It had been a little over four months since starting this journey and her sistership had sank. Everyone aboard The Aquarion had perished a fortnight ago at the hands of the sea as the ship sank into the briny depths.

If they were lucky, God would hear their prayers and reward their devotion by guiding them safely to their destination and providing for them upon landfall. She tucked away the leather-bound journal she had been using to keep records of the journey. As usual she didn't hear him enter the room. He was very skilled at entering a room undetected. He moved silently, but swiftly across the room to place his hand on her shoulder. As he did this, he leaned over and placed a gentle kiss upon her forehead. His wavy long dark blonde hair was falling down in front of his face and tickling her forehead. His memorizing blue eyes were like the ocean and looking into them made her want to dive in. "How are you feeling today my dearest?" She knew he was only asking as a formality because he could always sense how she was feeling. "Now that you have graced me with your presence, I am feeling much better, just a bit of sea sickness but you needn't worry about it my love." The last thing she wanted was for him to be concerned about the possibility of losing her. They had only been together for a less than a year, but they loved each other as deeply and passionately as if it had been decades. Life expectancies in these times weren't very long with the threat of illnesses constantly afoot, but when the inevitable happened she hoped they would find each other again. Their love would transcend the barriers of time. She stood to face him stretching her arm up to place her hand on his cheek. It was just a simple gesture, but it seemed to please him greatly. He let out a soft, but passion filled sigh of contentment. He brought his face down closer tilting his head slightly so that their noses were now brushing against each other. Her body shuttered in anticipation waiting for him to move his lips onto hers. When he finally did, she noticed a delightful tingling sensation. She didn't realize it at first, but he had lightly bitten her bottom lip. His hands were tangled in her hair now. He pulled away slowly, allowing her to steady her breath before kissing her one last time. As he leaned in to whisper something into her ear, she heard a noise Bzzzttt, Bzzzttt.Bzzzttt, Bzzzttt Bzzzttt, Bzzzttt.Bzzzttt, Bzzzttt.

Chapter Ten: Dream Interrupted

Bzzzttt, Bzzzttt. Bzzzttt, Bzzzttt Bzzzttt, Bzzzttt. Bzzzttt, Bzzzttt She groggily opened one eye. What was that noise? It took her brain a minute to realize that the it was the strange buzzing noise that she had heard at the end of her dream. She looked over just in time to save her phone which was set on vibrate and ringing was about to fall off her bedside table. Who could be interrupting her sleep at this hour? If it was Jaden, it better be an emergency.

Bzzzttt,Bzzzttt.Bzzzttt,BzzzttBzzzttt,Bzzzttt.Bzzzttt,Bzzzttt. The notification on the screen said "Probable Spam". She slid her finger over the ignore option. She chuckled to herself that smart phones had started thwarting spam callers by literally labeling them as spam. It was a mystery how spammers hadn't ceased to exist yet. In this day and age people weren't answering the phone when people they know called. Let alone people they didn't know.

Most work places these days knew to contact people her age over text. She looked over at the alarm clock to see that it wasn't as early as she thought it was. It was 9:45AM. Although it was her day off, at this point she might as well get up and go about her day. However, now that she was awake, she was kind of curious to know what the latest dream version of Mr. Eastman had wanted to whisper into her ear before she had woken up. Though the man in her dreams had long wavy locks and looked like Fabian; the male model from every romance cover in existence, she had still known it was him. His blue eyes were a dead giveaway; she still hadn't forgotten the way looking into them that night had made her feel. It was hard to imagine she would ever forget that feeling and if she was being honest with herself, she never wanted to. Jaden would find it hilarious that now she was adding wigs to Mr. Eastman in her dreams.

Her dreams were basically becoming soap operas with the way her subconscious was conjuring up images of him as if he was playing a brand-new character in each one. The next dream was probably going to have a big twist ending where his evil twin Nate would spring up out of nowhere and reveal that it was him she had married after he'd killed Noah the night of the rehearsal dinner. Then he'd wink at the camera as the voice-over started. Tune in tomorrow for an exciting new episode of As Shadow Ridge Turns!

Maybe she'd see what Jaden was up to later. He was probably still sleeping, but then again so would she if her phone hadn't woken her up. Both of them loved to sleep in on their off days. They would often joke that it was their reward for showing up to work every day like a responsible adult.

Right now, she needed to talk to Jaden to figure out what she was going to do about this crush, and do it fast. Jaden was her best friend, and even if talking about her dreams out loud was going to be embarrassing, he had more experience in the dating world than she did. He'd probably tell her to go for it, and maybe she should. She'd just have to figure out a way to see him again without seeming like she was too desperate for his attention.

The one thing she did know from all the years of reading Cool Teen! and all the other magazines with articles boasting " 7 Tips to Get a Guys Attention" was that most guys liked a woman who was approachable, but not too available. Too available was code for clingy. On television and movies guys would literally run in the opposite direction to get away from women they described as clingy.

What would she even wear if she visited the casino again? Last time she was dressed up because it was her birthday. That wasn't her usual style at all. Shouldn't she show up in her normal clothes so that if he was interested, he'd know what she looked like on a normal day? But if he was dressed in what she assumed was his normal attire that night, she might look ridiculous standing next to him on a future date. It's not as if she could afford to throw out her entire wardrobe and rack up thousands in credit card debt hoping that he might want to date her if she dressed better. This over-analyzation wasn't helping things at all.

Now she was creating fictional scenarios about him turning her down in her mind. Crazy and scary as it sounded, she had to see him again so she'd know if she had left any impression on him after their brief interaction. Hopefully he'd let her down easy if he didn't feel the same, or at least make up a believable lie about having some brand-new girlfriend. How was it even possible that a man who looked like him hadn't been snapped up yet? It was certainly in the realm of possibilities that being a wealthy casino owner might come with worries of people looking to get rich via marriage. She couldn't blame him at all if he was simply waiting for the right person to come along. Someone who would see past his money and love him for who he was as a person.

She'd spent her teenage years in her room dreaming about finding a guy who would be interested in her on more than just the surface level. The only person she had ever felt comfortable discussing her relationship goals with was Jaden. Other people would probably say she was wasting time waiting for a knight in shining armor to ride in on a horse and sweep her off to a castle and marry her. While that kind of thing made for a good animated princess movie it wasn't realistic in the least.

She picked out a pair of dark blue skinny jeans and a brand name t-shirt she'd found on sale at the mall a few years ago. After a quick breakfast of chocolate chip mini muffins and chocolate milk she brushed her teeth. It was after 10:30 so it was time to check off the next thing on the day's agenda. After establishing that Jaden was awake, she asked him if he'd like to hang out and talk for a little bit. He agreed and said he'd see her in 15 minutes after he finished getting dressed and ready for the day.

Shortly after that she heard a knock on her door so she got up to answer it. She didn't need to look out the little peephole in the door to know it was Jaden because he had a very specific knock. It was an original knock that they had made up together as teens. He could have let himself in with the key she had given him for emergency situations, but he preferred to knock before using the key. She didn't find that strange because she had an emergency key for his place and she did the same thing when she went over to his place. Regardless of the fact they had been best friends for over 6 years and trusted each other it was also good manners to announce oneself before barging in.

She let him in and then headed towards the kitchen. As she opened the refrigerator and grabbed a bottle of sweet tea for herself, she asked him, “Do you want something to drink?" She always kept around a few cans of Dr. Crush, Jaden's favorite soda just in case. "Sure, I'll take a Dr. Crush, if you have any" he responded. She grabbed one, and then checked the freezer to see if she had any ice. The bag was almost empty, but she had just enough for two glasses. She'd have to remember to pick some up at the store next time she went. She had a regular ice tray that she used in a pinch sometimes, but she preferred ice she didn't have to wait to freeze. Luckily for her, the grocery store carried bags of the chewy nugget ice that her and Jaden both loved getting in their fountain drinks at the gas station. She opened the cabinet next to the fridge and grabbed out two plastic glasses. She did have a few glass cups, but she didn't use them often. When she had moved into this apartment Jaden had bought her one of those four-piece glass dinner sets as a housewarming gift. Since they were fragile and had been given to her as a gift she tried to keep them safe by only using them for special occasions and holidays. The plastic cups were always on sale for fifty cents at the dollar store, and there was no risk of them breaking if she accidentally knocked one over. She could be a real klutz sometimes. She filled each glass with ice about halfway and then poured the drinks in. When she got back to the couch, she handed Jaden his glass. They both took a sip, and then set the glasses down on the cheap plastic coasters she had sitting on the table.

Chapter Eleven: Forming A Plan (Two Heads Are Better Than One)

For a while after he arrived, they talked about random things like a catchy new song Jaden had heard on the radio and upcoming movies that might be worth the drive to go watch. Then fortunately for her Jaden decided it was time to ask her what she had wanted to meet up and discuss.

"Let me guess. You need my help trying to figure out an inconspicuous way to see Hottie McBlueEyes again?" Jaden being an extrovert was one of the many things she appreciated about their friendship. He could help her navigate situations that made an introvert like her feel a lot less nervous.

"Yes, I've been trying to figure out for weeks how to see him again and put myself out there. I don't want to look like a fool in case he doesn't even remember me." When she finished what she had to say she pulled her legs up onto the couch and put her head on her knees.

She knew he wouldn't judge her, but it still felt a little embarrassing that she was making such a big deal over a guy. Gushing over male celebrities with him was one thing, but the gorgeous casino owner she barely knew was a different story.

"Of course I'll help! What are best friends for if they don't come up a clever plan to help their best friend bag a hottie? Girl if he can't see what a catch you are it's his loss not yours." He shrugged his shoulders and then moved closer to her and gave her a side hug.

She lifted her head and cracked a little smile when he said the last part. He always knew what to say or do to cheer her up. He was deep in thought with one of his arms propped up on the couch and the other on his knee with his hand resting underneath his chin. He reminded her of one of those philosopher statues. It was the classic pose he did whenever he was trying to come up with an idea. A few minutes later he looked at her, his blue eyes lighting up like fireworks on The Fourth of July.

He started to speak barely holding in excitement as he started explaining the plan. "Here it goes. It's the perfect way for you to go to the back to the casino and possibly run into him again. Next week we'll go together and you can donate some blood. While you do that I'll walk around and play a few slots. Hopefully he's the type of boss who walks around the place checking up on things. If I see him, I'll send you a message letting you know."

Lucy nodded her head in agreement her eyes wide as she hung on every word he said listening carefully as if her life depended on it. Which if she couldn't do something about this crush it just might or at least that is how it felt.

Jaden could see how carefully Lucy was listening to him, so he took a moment to reflect before continuing. "Then I'll "casually" run into him and strike up a conversation. You'll come up, say hello and then I'll ask him if he'd be interested in joining us for a quick drink. I'll make an excuse that I have to step away for a minute and you'll stay and talk to him. While I do that you ask if he'd like to join you for dinner sometime. If he says yes, you'll share a meal, make him fall in love and the two of you will live happily ever after."

A brilliant plan indeed. While the plan did involve her mustering up enough courage to ask Mr. Eastman to dinner it did sound like a good plan. Donating blood was a good deed. It also happened to be something that Mr. Eastman cared deeply about. She was a bit nervous because she had never donated blood before. In high school there was a blood drive and she had signed up for it, but she'd recently pierced her ears again less than sixth months prior. As a result, she couldn't donate and she hadn't really thought about it since then. Come to think of it she didn't even know her own blood type. This wasn't unusual. Most people probably didn't know theirs either. There had been exactly two people she went to school with that wore medical alert bracelets with their blood types listed. Other than that people didn't go around shouting their private medical info from the rooftops.

"Kudos to you on coming up with a plan that should be easy enough for me to follow. I am a little nervous about the blood donation part, but it'll be fine. The dinner invite will be trickier, but with you nearby I'll manage somehow. I'll watch some breathing exercises online to prepare if I have to."

Jaden was beaming with pride as a wide toothy grin started to spread across his face. He took her hands in his as he repeated the words of encouragement he'd said to her many years ago when she was crying on his shoulder trying to forget the sting of her first and only breakup. "You've got this! Always remember you are beautiful inside and out, and don't ever let any man make you forget that."

Now that the plan was in order they could just hang and watch tv for a little while before Jaden had to leave. She grabbed the remote and turned on the TV. There were a few free streaming apps to choose from, but she started with Neptune TV! which showed reruns from a few older shows they liked to watch. After browsing through for a few minutes, she decided to find an episode of Clarrisa, The Teenage Sorceress. The show was about the adventures of a teenage girl and her two aunts that had magical powers they had to keep hidden. Things were complicated by the hijinks of Clarrisa's cat Shadow, a three-hundred-year-old warlock who had been transformed into a cat as punishment for revealing his magical powers to a human. After they had watched two episodes Jaden had some errands to run so he hugged her and told her he'd see her at work.

Chapter Twelve:

Running Errands

Speaking of errands, today was as good as any for her to make that trip to the grocery store. She turned off the TV and got ready to leave. Before she could head out she'd have to find her keys. She grabbed her purse off the counter and started searching. It took her a moment because the keys had fallen to the very bottom of her purse. Whenever she went looking for them it seemed they were always hidden underneath everything else. Her theory was that finding a set of keys when you needed them was like trying to find that last penny in your wallet at the store when paying with exact change. The penny was definitely in there somewhere, but it was always stuck or hiding in some nook or cranny. If there was a line behind you it was always nerve wracking. Then it was like trying to look for buried treasure with a dull shovel and a huge hole in the map.

As she left, she locked the door behind her. When she got outside, she used a second key to lock the deadbolt as an added precaution. Despite the fact she had just turned the key and heard the click of the deadbolt locking she still jiggled the door handle to make sure it was locked. Finding her car was a much easier task than finding her keys. Each tenant had a reserved spot with their apartment number painted onto the concrete. The numbers were super easy to see because the painters had used school bus yellow spray-paint.

In total there were 40 apartments broken up into 5 units with a number followed by A or B. All of the A apartments were downstairs and the Bs were upstairs. Her apartment number was 16A. Jaden's was 18A. Somehow, they had both lucked into being downstairs and neither of their upstairs neighbors were very loud. Hers was a night shift worker at a factory a few towns over so he was asleep during the day and gone at night. She wasn't entirely sure of his name, but she was pretty sure his work shirt had the name Tyler embroidered on it. She had rarely seen the lady that lived above Jaden, but she'd never heard any loud music or noise when she was over there. Neither one of them knew much about the rest of the neighbors. Everyone kept to themselves, which was fine by her.

It beat the alternative option that inspired reality TV shows like Neighbors From Hell and Neighbors Gone Wild: Crazy& Unhinged. The preview for the episode of Neighbors From Hell airing this week showed a lady fighting with a neighbor who enjoyed dumping her cat's used litter on her neighbor's front porch. In a different clip it showed a guy fist fighting with a neighbor after catching the neighbor keying and then throwing shaving cream all over his brand-new car. The popularity of shows like that made her really appreciative of the fact that she didn't have to deal with neighbors like that.

Fifteen minutes later Lucy arrived at the grocery store Save-A-Bunch. It was smaller than the chain stores like Andersonn's and Wilmart, but it had decent prices and quality food. It didn't occur to her until she got inside that she probably should have made a list before going to the store, but it was too late to worry about that now. The only thing she knew she needed was ice, but she could grab that on the way out. If she grabbed it now by the time she made it to the checkout counter it would probably be melted like a snowman on a 75° day. Since she had no clue what she actually needed, she decided to start in the frozen food aisle. There was always something she could find there.

As she walked down the aisle the garlic bread caught her eye. She grabbed a box with pre-sliced loaves and placed it in her cart. Now she needed to figure out what type of pasta she wanted to go with it, but shed have to go to a different aisle for that. She walked a little bit further and found a cheesy potato and rice skillet meal. Now it was time to head to the dry goods aisle to grab a box of pasta. After picking up a box of thin spaghetti and meat flavored marina sauce she had everything for at least one night of dinner. A little further down the aisle she spotted one of those dinner in a box complete meal option that had biscuits, chicken, and mashed potatoes. Another quick and easy meal checked off the list. As she started to step out of the aisle with her cart another customer came zooming out of nowhere with their cart.

"Hey watch it Orangutan!" the person shouted.

Upon closer inspection she noticed that underneath the unkept mountain man beard, modified mullet, and confederate flag shirt was one of her former classmates, Jimmy Lee. No big surprise that even after graduating he was still a bigot. In school he had proudly talked about how his heritage could be traced back to Robert E. Lee. It didn't happen as often these days, but she still got stares and heard the occasional racially motivated slur from idiotic townsfolk like the unevolved specimen standing in front of her. What she really wanted to respond back to this imbecile was that he was a complete dumb-ass who needed to watch where he was going and to get over a war that was lost well over a century ago, but instead she just kept walking.

She was well aware that saying nothing wasn't going to help stop racism in the world, but he looked like the type that had a certain white hooded outfit in his closet. That type of racist was completely unpredictable and dangerous so for her own safety it was best not to retaliate. She figured the best thing to do was just keep walking which seemed to be effective because he didn't engage with her further. After searching a few more aisles and adding a bag of baked pickle chips, mini pretzels, a box of chocolate chip cookies, and a gallon of Blue Diamond Sweet Tea she was ready to check out. As she headed towards the checkout area, she could see that only one register was open and who else but Jimmy Lee was in line waiting. That was just her luck. Hopefully, he wouldn't notice her because she didn't want to deal with anymore of his stupidity. Thankfully just as she had she started to get into the line, the light on the "15 items or less" lit up so she moved over and put her all of her items on the checkout counter.

Before beginning the transaction the cashier Mark asked, "Do you have a Save-A-Bunch card? If you do please enter the number or scan your card before I start ringing up your items."

She quickly scanned her card and as he began ringing up her items she asked, "Can I add a bag of ice too? Please and thank you."

Mark responded, "You're welcome, it's no problem at all. Would you like the 10 lb. bag or the 7 lb. small bag? Regular cubes or Chewy Nugget? The regular bags are on sale today for $1.75 "

Lucy thought about it for a moment before answering. On one hand the bag of small regular ice was cheaper, but she did prefer the chewy nugget ice. "I'll take one small bag of chewy nugget ice please and thank you."

Mark scanned a barcode near the register to add the ice and told her the final total and that using her card had saved her $1.50. She put her card into the card reader and entered her pin to pay. After checking to make sure all her bags were in the cart she exited through glass doors and grabbed a bag of ice on her way to the car.

Once she was back in her car, she checked her side and rearview mirrors to make sure that it was safe to back out. When she had established that it was clear she slowly backed out and drove toward the exit. When she got into the turning lane she flicked on her turn signal and waited until she could safely pull out onto the street. When the traffic had cleared enough for her to go, she turned her steering wheel to the left and got into the right lane. She had to wait a minute for the light to turn green, but when it did, she went through and stayed on the main road until she got back to the road she needed to turn onto to get back to her apartment.

Upon arriving back at her apartment, she grabbed the bags from the backseat and went inside to unload them. When she was finished with that, she watched some TV and then when it was closer to dinner time, she got the stuff back out to make spaghetti. First, she grabbed a pot out, and filled it with water and some salt. Then she turned the oven on and set it to 375°. Next, she turned on the front burner and let the water reach a boil. When it was boiling, she carefully added the spaghetti noodles and left it to cook stirring and checking it occasionally until it was soft but not mushy. The oven had finished preheating so she tossed three slices of garlic bread onto the pan and set a timer for five minutes. While the noodles were cooking, she grabbed out a small pot, poured the marinara sauce in and put it onto the back burner on low to warm up.

She grabbed the strainer out of the dish rack, strained the pasta, then put it back onto the stove and added the marinara. She used a ladle to grab some pasta and placed it onto the plate. When the garlic bread was done, she pulled the pan out and let it cool for a minute before adding it to the plate. The finishing touch was sprinkling some parmesan onto the top and then it was finally time to eat. After finishing her meal, she washed the dishes she had used and then watched three episodes of Ruthless Kitchen before showering and preparing for bed.

Chapter Thirteen:

Getting Ready

Beep!Beep!Beep! The sound of her alarm going off was more shrill and irritating than usual. She opened one eye just enough to see the clock said 5:00AM and used one finger to press the button to turn it off. She groggily sat up and placed both of her feet on the ground. When she felt awake enough to stand up, she slowly walked towards the restroom. The toilet made a loud series of noises after she flushed it. Whoosh! Clink-floosh!

She moved to the sink and turned the handles until the water was at a comfortable temperature. She stuck her hands underneath the stream of warm water to wet them and then grabbed the bottle of hand soap and pumped it two times. With her hands lathered she started rubbing them together making sure to clean in between her fingers. La dee dum, la dee dum, la dee dum she hummed as she twisted her hands back and forth over one another to ensure her palms were clean. When she was finished, she grabbed a piece of paper towel from the paper towel holder mounted to the wall. After her hands were dry, she used a piece of paper towel to turn off the water.

When she returned to her room she rifled through her drawers and grabbed out a work shirt and pants. She lifted up the shirt and pulled it over her head and down over her neck. She slipped her left arm up and out of the sleeve and then the right. Next, she slipped off her boy shorts underwear and pulled a fresh pair up and over her hips. Then she sat on the bed and put on a pair of pants slipping her left leg in first and then her right standing to finish pulling them up. She slipped a pair of socks on and headed into the kitchen to grab a bite to eat.

First, she grabbed a bowl from the cabinet, milk from the fridge, and the cereal box off the counter. The last step was pouring some Choco-puffs about halfway and stirring it to make sure every puff was covered. Crunch! Crunch! Crunch! She chewed each bite carefully savoring the chocolatey goodness of each bite. When she was finished, she lifted the bowl to her lips and slurped down the chocolate flavored milk. After quickly washing the bowl, she set it in on the dry rack and went into the bathroom to brush her teeth and finish getting ready. She quickly slipped on her shoes, locked the door, and set off for work.

After a hectic week at work dealing with almost 500 guests per day, and hundreds of customers in the gift shop she was ready to enjoy her night off. Tonight, they were headed back to the casino to put Jaden's plan in action. Currently she was looking through her entire wardrobe trying to find an outfit to wear. This was proving to be harder than she expected. She wanted to create the perfect look that would be classy enough to catch Mr. Eastmans attention, but not stray too far from her regular laid-back style. Finally, after what felt like she'd been searching forever, she managed to find a light pink v neck summer blouse with a butterfly design. There were small butterflies of various colors spread throughout, as if they were majestically flying through the air. She didn't even remember when or where she had found this shirt, but she tried it on and it looked cute enough. After pairing it with some dark blue skinny jeans and a pair of black flats with thin ankle straps her look was almost complete.

As far as makeup was concerned a little bit of mascara, eyeliner, and lip gloss was going to have to do the job. Although she admired the skills of people who could do their makeup and end up looking like a beautiful work of art, she was not one of those people. The birthday look she had considered "glam" had nothing on the transformative results some people had. However, looking in the mirror she realized it wasn't worth dwelling on. Becoming an entirely new person to suit the tastes of someone she barely knew wasn't a habit she ever wanted to form.

Eventually she would grow old, and a relationship built entirely around physical beauty was unlikely to last forever. If they hit it off, Mr. Eastman would just have to base his feelings for her on what he would be seeing on a regular basis. Bzzzttt, Bzzzttt. She looked at her phone and saw Jaden had sent a text saying he was outside by her car waiting. She replied that she would be out in a minute. As she stepped out the door, she decided that tonight no matter how nervous she was she was going to shoot her shot.

It was high time that she stopped worrying about the what ifs of life and started taking chances and seeing where that would lead. She climbed into the driver's seat and buckled her seat beat. Once Jaden was all situated in the passenger seat, she put her key in the ignition and started the car. Jaden fiddled with the radio dial until he settled on a catchy song he described as "words of wisdom for going after what you want." She turned up the volume and listened to the lyrics hoping they would provide her with the inspiration she needed to be brave.

Chapter Fourteen: When Good Deeds Go Bad

Once they were inside the casino they made a beeline for the door to the blood donation room. Jaden walked her to the door and wished her good luck as he went to go work on his part of the plan. When she walked in the room she was greeted by a friendly nurse named Nora who asked her for her license and told her to take a seat and fill out some paperwork. After she was finished Nora came over to double check everything had been filled out properly and handed her back her license. Following the verbal confirmation of her name and birth date the last step was answering a few medical history questions for Nora.

"We're almost ready to start, I see you've never donated before so I'm going to walk you through what's going to happen. First I have to check your temperature, blood pressure, pulse, and hemoglobin levels and if everything looks good your donation will be ready to be collected." She started scribbling on her clipboard as she talked, showing how many times, she had done this that it seemed like second nature to her.

When everything was good to go, Norah fixed the privacy sheet in front of them and told her to sit or relax on the hospital bed. Lucy decided that lying back was probably the better option in case she passed out or something, but hopefully she wouldn't. After the Area was properly cleansed Norah inserted a new sterilized needle into her arm. It felt like a quick pinch, but after that it didn't hurt. The whole process took about ten minutes and then a bandage was placed on her arm and Nora thanked her for her donation and gave her some post donation instructions to follow. She sat up and Nora handed her a small bottle of apple juice and a bag of pretzels to eat while she waited fifteen minutes to make sure she'd be fine to leave the room.

There was no one else waiting so Nora had told her it was fine to wait a few extra minutes if she wanted so she waited twenty minutes. Things felt completely normal, but as she opened the door to leave, she suddenly felt lightheaded and then her legs buckled underneath her as she started to pass out.

Her eyes were barely open and she felt a little dizzy, the last thing she remembered was falling towards the ground. Her head didn't hurt though so thankfully someone had caught her before she hit the ground. She felt a slight jostling motion and realized whoever it was carrying her somewhere. At the moment she didn't care who it was, all she wanted to do was regain enough strength to get up and leave. Hopefully Jaden had been nearby and he hadn't seen Mr. Eastman.

The mere thought of him seeing her in this weakened state was nightmare fuel. The person gently placed her down and then she could feel someone's fingers on her wrist. Then she heard a woman's voice say her pulse is fine. She realized that she must be back on the bed in the donation room and the voice was Nora's. Then she heard two other voices speaking in hushed tones. One of the voices she recognized as Jaden's. Her mind still felt kind of fuzzy so she wasn't sure who the other voice belonged to. She tried to open her eyes fully but she still felt weak. The figure was blurry but through the small slits of vision she could swear she saw a tall blonde-haired person. Maybe she had passed out while donating blood and this whole thing was just a hallucination. She tried to move her arms so she could slide up into a sitting position. She heard Jaden's voice and the other persons come closer as she felt two people helping grab her to help move her into a sitting position.

After a few minutes she finally felt strong enough to open her eyes. As her vision came back into focus the first thing she saw was his piercing blue eyes staring back at her. His eyebrows were furrowed causing small lines to form across his forehead. His lips were tightened and his arms were crossed in concern. This wasn't at all how she had imagined seeing him again.

Jaden was the first to speak. "How are you feeling? You really scared me. I was in the middle of talking to Mr. Eastman and then I looked over and saw you falling. Lucky for you Mr. Eastman went into hyperdrive and practically flew across the room in time to catch you. Then he carried you onto the bed and now you're awake and all caught up."

She covered her face with her hands in embarrassment. As if it wasn't bad enough, he had actually seen her fall, he had also carried her in his arms like a baby. While she was grateful that he had quickly jumped into action to save her now he probably thought of her as a damsel in distress. At least she hadn't woken up to him leaning over her with his seductive lips pressed against hers like she'd seen in every animated princess movie in existence. When and if he ever kissed her after this, she wanted to be fully alert and prepared for it.

She needed to thank him, and do it fast before she got too nervous and started blabbering on.

"Thank you for all your help, Mr. Eastman. I guess it turns out I was more nervous about giving blood than I had anticipated. Nora had double checked to make sure that I was fine before I left. I swear I felt completely normal. Until I didn't. I felt myself start to pass out and then I was falling. I'm very grateful that you were able to catch me before I hit the ground, but I'm very sorry you had to see that, and then ya know carry me in your arms like a newborn into this room."

Just when she thought to herself that she had managed to keep her cool her nerves took over and words started tumbling out uncontrollably. "I know that we barely know each other and you're so far out of my league it's not funny, but I had wanted to ask you to grab dinner with me sometime. I wasn't even sure if you'd remember me, and now that I've made a fool of myself, I know you probably will, but for all the wrong reasons. I really wouldn't blame you if you said you never wanted to see me again. Look at me rambling on. Sorry if I inconvenienced you. Your night has probably been ruined and I'm so embarrassed I might never show my face in here ever again." When she was done speaking, she felt like she wanted to crawl into a cave, change her identity and live like a hermit for the rest of her life.

She looked over at Jaden whose face looked shocked. His jaw looked like it was on the floor and his eyes were as big as saucers. (His shock was partially due to the fact that he did not know if he should be laughing or pitying his best friend as she embarrassed herself right in front of him and the guy she liked.) She couldn't blame him for being stunned because she hadn't been prepared for the words that had come out of her own mouth. As for Mr. Eastman's reaction she had no clue. Since the moment she had finished uttering the last words she had been avoiding eye contact with him. Before Jaden could say anything to try and help her save face Mr. Eastman started speaking. His sensuous voice providing a momentary distraction from her awkwardness.

"Please call me Noah. I think that after carrying someone in your arms like a newborn as you described it, we've gotten close enough for you to use my first name."

He did have a point. However, she wished he hadn't repeated the phrase she had used, but damn if the words didn't sound sultry the way he said them.

As he continued on, she noticed the corners of his mouth starting to turn upward and form a smile that revealed a row of perfectly glistening teeth.

"In regards to your remark about me being out of your league I strongly disagree with that statement. In hope this doesn't sound too forward, but your exquisite beauty astonished me the night we met."

Her mind was racing trying to process the revelation that he had been thinking about her. Specifically, how beautiful he thought she was. Maybe she hadn't woken up yet. This was all just a lucid dream and he was saying exactly what her subconscious wanted him to say. She couldn't help it; she had to pinch her arm to make sure. She felt a stinging sensation and her skin was a light red in the spot she had pinched. At least now she had confirmation this wasn't a dream.

A smirk crossed Noah's face as he let out a "heh" and began to speak again in a hypnotic tone.

"I assure you Miss Lofthouse this is not a dream. Though the circumstances are much different than you had imagined, I will gladly accept your dinner invitation. Shall I meet you there or pick you up for the occasion? Dealer's choice.

Lucy looked quizzical for a moment thinking about what Mr. Eastman had just said. Her mind was still not entirely back to normal and she probably looked confused because her mind was still trying to process the words he was saying.

“Sorry, a bit of casino humor. I meant to say that I do not wish to make you uncomfortable therefore the decision is up to you." Mr. Eastman responds while looking at her with those blue eyes making her head spin even more.

He handed her a business card with a direct line to his office, and told her to get back to him when she had finalized a plan. She took it and shoved it in her pocket.

"I am glad to see that you are feeling better, but I'm sure that you are most eager to get home and rest. Mr. Evans has assured me that he will see to it that you arrive home safely. I look forward to our dinner. Goodnight, Miss Lofthouse."

As he turned to walk away, she extended her hand towards his and grabbed it. It was a bolder move than she would normally make, but tonight was about taking chances. She could tell by his face that this took him a little by surprise, but he just stood there letting her hold his hand. She looked directly into his eyes that were as endless as the horizon and blue as a clear lake on a summer's day.

"Hey Noah, if you want me to use your first name, you're going to have to call me Lucy from now on. No more of this Miss Lofthouse business. Though I will admit hearing you say it does make my heart skip a beat."

Jaden snort laughed when she said that last part. By this point he probably thought she was off her rocker. Admittedly she was acting very uncharacteristically. He gave her a thumbs up signal though so he approved of her newfound bravery.

"Ja, godnatt min älskling, Lucy".

He smiled as he said it. Although she didn't understand what Noah had said she assumed it was some form of yes followed by her name. She was definitely going to have to ask him what language he was speaking or use her phone to detect the language. She wasn't complaining though. He sounded even more alluring and looked twice as handsome when he spoke in what she assumed was his native tongue. She released his hand which she hadn't realized she was still holding and he moved towards the door. On his way out he called back to Jaden.

"Godnatt, Mr. Evans."

When Noah was out of earshot Jaden gave her a high five and congratulated her on successfully completing the mission then playfully ribbed her a little about the improvisation. Then it was time to leave. As they went to walk out the door they were met by Barry who informed them that he had been requested by Noah to walk them out to her car. Jaden drove them back to her apartment and offered to stay the night and sleep on the couch so he could make sure she was fine. The second her head hit the pillow she was out like a light.

Chapter Fifteen: Chaos In Times Of Work

The next week at work was a blur. Just as Matt had predicted rooms were nearly sold out every day. The paychecks were good, but the busier the place got the worse guests attitudes seemed to get. She couldn't pinpoint the exact reason, maybe it was the combination of too many people in one place or travel tips telling people to throw hissy fits to get discounts, but there was a definitely a correlation of some sort.

Two days ago, a lady had gotten in her face over being told to pay for a soft drink from the drink machine after the free breakfast was over. Yesterday a man had broken a shot glass and got pissed off when he was told that he would need to pay $4.99 for it. Apparently, it was absolutely ridiculous to expect him to pay full price for a broken item. An item which wasn't broken until he was goofing off and knocked it off the shelf.

Jaden's week wasn't going much better. A guest had demanded a refund for food that was described as absolutely atrocious, but there was only one bite left on the plate. Seeing as how Shawn was the one that cooked it, she couldn't say for sure the guest was lying about it not being the best, but it was a little suspicious that the food was 99% gone before the person complained.

Another guest had gotten mad because they tried to bring their own cooler of outside food into the restaurant and eat it. If it had been one person with an allergy issue bringing their own food nothing would have been said, but it was a whole family of six. Matt had been called to come speak with them because they could not understand why bringing ham and cheese sandwiches, bags of chips, and soft drinks from home was a no go at a restaurant. Their reasoning was that there was plenty of space in the restaurant so what did it matter. As Matt explained to them it wasn't an issue of space it was an issue of bringing outside food into a place that served food that they could purchase. One expletive filled rant and a threat to get the police involved later they finally admitted defeat and decided to eat outside.

Lucy picked up the phone growing more nervous with every ring. After the fifth ring Noah picked up the phone. His voice sounded firm and confident.

"Hello, Noah Eastman speaking. May I ask who is calling and what this is in regards to?" Hearing his voice on the other line she realized that she didn't actually know what she was going to say.

It's not as if she had prior experience calling up handsome guys who had agreed to go out with her. Especially one whose voice held her attention over the phone just as strongly as it did in person. Next time she was definitely writing out a script to follow. Oh yeah, she still hadn't answered his question. She needed to say something or he'd probably think it was a prank caller because all he had heard up to this point was the sound of someone breathing on the other end.

Her voice was dripping with insecurity as she started to speak."Ummm...You gave me your business card last week. This is Lofty Lucehouse. I mean wait..let me start over, I'm so friggin terrible at this. I've never done this before. You'd think in twenty-one years I'd have learned how to talk on the phone."

She brought her palm up to her face silently cringing in embarrassment at the fact that she had already fumbled this phone call so badly. She imagined his face on the other end was one of bewilderment. He was probably fighting back laughter at this exact moment. He was just being professional and resisting the urge. What if he was regretting the dinner invite? Several scenarios were flashing through her mind in quick succession. She needed to get herself together and finish this phone call with some semblance of dignity.

"Hello Noah, this is Lucy Lofthouse. I'm sorry if I bothered you. I was calling to finalize our plan to go out for dinner. If you still want to go. I mean I hope you do, but if you've changed your mind after this phone call it's fine." She heard the sound of a chuckle on the other end.

Was that a good or bad sign? Had she messed things up and now he was trying to figure out how to let her down gently? There was silence on the other end for only a moment, but it felt like a lifetime.

"You haven't messed anything up Ms. Lofthouse. I mean Lucy. I find your nervousness endearing. This call has not changed my mind about going out to dinner with you. I've been looking forward to your call. Have you decided if you want to meet at the restaurant or shall I pick you up at your residence? Only if you feel comfortable giving me the address of course." Then once again there was silence on the other end of the line.

She was ecstatic that he was still interested in going on a date with her. Despite her obvious inexperience on the phone and with relationships in general. How did she get so fortunate that a nervous wreck like her had managed to capture the attention of a man with the patience of a saint? Most men would have thrown in the towel after the blood donation incident. Which she was still trying to forget, but while she found it embarrassing it had also felt really good. He barely knew her, and yet he was strangely protective of her. Then again, she still couldn't completely explain her own feelings towards him.

Nothing about their relationship was normal, but maybe that was the secret to finding one's soul mate. It was rare, but she wanted to believe that soulmates existed. They most certainly did in the animal world. Maybe he was her penguin. It wasn't about how long you had known the person. It was going on awkward first dates that turned into relationships and weddings and eventually growing old together. There was time to worry about those things later. Right now, she needed to answer his question and wrap up this phone call.

"There's this new Italian restaurant that just opened up in Moon Hollow last month. I've been hearing a lot of good things about it so far. You can pick me up at my apartment at 6:00, it's totally fine for you to have the address. Then we'll head over to the restaurant together. Obviously. That's what happens when two people are in the same vehicle. If you don't like Italian food we can go always go someplace else." While she waited for his response it occurred to her that she wasn't sure what type of food was best to eat on first dates.

She had panicked and thrown out an idea based upon the fact that Italian food was seen as romantic in movies she'd seen. Even cartoon dogs were known to fall in love after sharing some spaghetti. There had also been a large advertisement for Pasta Garden, the new restaurant in this week's newspaper. If he didn't like Italian food, she would just leave picking the place up to him.

"If the lady wishes to eat Italian food, then we shall have Italian food. Next Friday at 6:00PM sharp I will arrive to take you out. Pardon me if this is too forward, but hearing your voice which sounds as sweet as honey has given me immense pleasure. I am eternally grateful that you walked into my establishment and reignited my passion for a life outside the walls of my casino. Apologies Lucy, but I must end this call now and make a business call. Goodnight, Miss Lofthouse."

Chapter Sixteen: Insecurities

Dinner plans had been finalized and Noah had business to attend to so she said a quick goodbye and hung up the phone. Her heart fluttered in her chest. She officially had a date. Disbelief is not a strong enough word to describe how she was feeling about having a date next Friday. If someone had told her two months ago that she would be having dinner with a man that looked like Noah Eastman she would've scoffed. Laughed directly in their face at the thought that someone like him had any interest in her. He was confident, drop dead gorgeous, and tall. Meanwhile she was bashful, ordinary, and petite.

While Noah seemed quite impressed by her looks it was still hard for her to see herself in the same light. Her relationship with her body image was complicated. When she was a child people had teased her about being thin and shapeless.

Until puberty hit and did a number on her. At 13, seemingly overnight she went from wearing one of those cutesy training bras in the juniors' section to having stretchmarks and c cups and by high school she was a dd. Creeps and young guys alike would often stare at her chest, but in the case of the older guys she found it disturbing and gross. There was no mistaking that she was underage. The younger guys were dealing with hormones of their own so to an extent it was understandable. Gross, but understandable. Although she still wished they cared more about her personality than the two mountains underneath her shirt.

In addition to being self-conscious about the stretch marks on her chest she also had them on her arms and stomach. Her face also became acne prone which was annoying and difficult to manage. Considering that society was always pushing the narrative that being attractive meant being model thin and having flawless skin coming to terms with her body had proven to be difficult. With the help of a skin care line developed by a duo of dermatologists her acne issues were more controlled, but she still had dark spots as reminders of when it hadn't been under control.

Despite what it sounds like, there were certain aspects she had learned to appreciate. People had often complimented her curly hair which looked shoulder length due to shrinkage, but was halfway down her back when it was straightened. Although she rarely straightened it these days because the process took several hours and then the second any humidity was introduced the curls would start to reform. She also received a lot of compliments on her eye color. Someone had once described them as "a rich brown hue comparable to freshly melted milk chocolate. Friday night had finally arrived. Noah had called earlier to confirm the address and he was on his way to ger place now. She looked in the mirror one last time for a "fit check" as Jaden called it.

She was wearing a turquoise butterfly sleeve scoop neck top that had a chain going across the neckline and a removable belt that went across her waistline. She paired the shirt with black leggings and a pair of plain black canvas shoes. Jaden had helped her find the shirt online. It was already on sale for 25%

off, and she had saved a little bit of additional money by using the $15 cash back rewards from her credit card. Between the original sale price and the $15 off from using her credit card she had only ended up paying $20 which according to Jaden was a very good deal. The black leggings and canvas shoes were something she already owned.

Her makeup for the night was pretty basic. Turquoise eyeshadow, mascara, black eyeliner, and lip gloss completed her "first date" look. She had already sent a photo to Jaden to see what he thought of her look. Once he had given it his seal of approval, she wasn't worried. As her best friend she trusted that he would tell her if she looked ridiculous. He had no qualms whatsoever about telling her what the homemade Halloween costume she made sophomore year had looked like. He had truly saved her from a lifetime of embarrassment. To this day she still cringed just thinking about that disastrous outfit. Since she wasn't sure how the bill would be handled because she had technically invited him on the date, she had a little bit of cash and her credit card just in case. Her wallet was in a little black clutch purse that she had found one of the times she'd went to the mall with Jaden.

In between messaging Jaden who was trying to calm her nerves about her date, she kept looking out the window to see if

Noah had arrived yet. Around the hundredth time she had looked out she saw him pull up in a sleek black luxury car. She wasn't good with identifying the make or model of a car on sight. She only knew hers because she was the owner, and Jaden's because she had been there when he had bought it. Noah stepped out of his car and started walking towards her apartment door.

The first thing she noticed was what he was wearing. She didn't know why she had expected him to show up in a suit. They were going on a first date, not a business meeting. He looked rebellious in a black leather jacket paired with a dark maroon v neck shirt and dark blue jeans. As dashing as his looks were when he was in a suit this versatile bad boy look he going for was giving that look a run for its money. Before he could knock on her door, she stepped out to meet him. He greeted her with one of his signature charming smiles. She could tell he was trying not to be obvious about it, but his eyes were surveying her. He was paying attention to every small detail like an artist trying to recreate a masterpiece from memory. She thought about jokingly telling him to take a picture because it would last longer, but he'd probably pull out his phone and pretend to do it just to mess with her. Or say he'd wink at her then say something witty like "only if you take your clothes off first," and then laugh his head off as she got all flustered by his comment.

He stepped closer to her and started to speak. "Miss Lofthouse, you look absolutely magnificent tonight. In all my years I have never beheld such a beautiful sight. " He held his hand out to her, and she took it allowing him to walk her to the passenger side and open the door for her.

As she climbed in, she thought to herself that not only was he the most attractive man she'd even seen he was also a gentleman. Not that she would have complained if he hadn't opened her door. In these modern times a woman could open a car door all by herself if she wanted. As he climbed in the driver's side she noticed the smell of his cologne. Rich and earthy yet not over powering. Just like his outfit it suited him well. He asked if she had a preference for the radio station, but she was agreeable to almost anything so she let him pick. It was his car after all. After pushing the button to scan through the various stations he settled on a station that boasted about playing today's hits and yesterday's classics. When they arrived at Pasta Garden he parked, went around to her door and opened it giving her his hand as she climbed out.

When they were inside, he gave the hostess his last name and they were seated at a corner table near the window. The lighting was dim and created an atmosphere of intimacy. Considering how nice this restaurant was she hoped the prices wouldn't be outrageous. The waitress appeared and brought a basket of bread to the table. Then she handed them regular menus and a wine menu. Her dinner plans and bank account had not accounted for wine. She assumed he either must not like wine or he sensed she was worried about the prices because he said no thanks and continued looking at the menu. The waitress took their drink order and she got a raspberry sweet tea and he ordered a water. There were plenty of pasta options but she decided to try something besides spaghetti. In the end she decided to go with four cheese manicotti and garlic bread. Noah ordered a stuffed Chicken Marsala, but no garlic bread. He explained that he preferred regular rolls because garlic bread gave him heartburn.

As they were waiting for their food to arrive, she decided that she should probably ask him some questions. She didn't know where to start but she figured that gathering some general info was the best way to go.

She started with a simple question." So, Noah, where are you from?"

He waited a moment as if he was trying to figure out the best answer. "As I'm sure you've noticed my accent I will start by answering that I am originally from Sigtuna, Sweden. Though throughout the years I have also lived in Stockholm and many other cities and countries. Swedish is my native tongue, but I lived in Paris for many years, so I am also fluent in French. Now I believe it is my turn to ask you a question."

"Tell me Lucy, have you always lived in Shadow Ridge?"

Lucy paused before answering. "I have lived in Shadow Ridge since I was five, but I was born in a Northern Indiana town called Frostford.

“My turn.” Now that she knew where he was from, it was time to figure out the answer to another question that had been on her mind since she met him. He looked maybe late 20s at most. "How old are you?"

With the most serious expression she had ever seen he answered "1,077 years old, but I look good for my age, don't I? Nobody would guess that I'm a day over 28. I had dinner with William Shakespeare while he was writing Hamlet."

She was right in the middle of taking a drink when he said it. If only he knew how close she had been to spitting out her drink. Now that would have been embarrassing. Apparently, he had gotten tickled by his own joke because he couldn't help letting out a burst of laughter after immediately following the last sentence. Obviously, his actual age was 28, but she could play along with his joke.

It was her turn to get him good. "Interesting, with those laugh lines and the crow's feet I wouldn't have dreamed you were a day over 35."

The look on his face when she said that was priceless. She felt like pulling out her phone to take a photo of the moment she had rendered the jokester speechless.

She slapped her knee and threw her head back in laughter before continuing on. "I'm sorry, I had to do it. I knew you were joking so I couldn't resist making one of my own. I just wanted to see your reaction when I said it." Just as she finished speaking their food arrived.

Noah cracked a smile so things were still good. She didn't know how she would've handled it if he had taken her seriously. He was right she never would have guessed that he was 28, but that wasn't a problem. They were both adults, and if things progressed between them, she didn't care about whether or not seven years was too big of an age gap.

The waitress had brought a bowl of salad to their table when she delivered the food so Lucy grabbed the tongs and placed a pile of salad on one of the small plates that had been brought with the salad. It was pre-tossed in Caesar dressing and had lots of croutons and parmesan. Ceaser dressing was her favorite. The aroma of the various spices in the marinara sauce on her manicotti was mouthwatering.

She took a bite and let out a small "mmmm" noise.

Noah seemed to be enjoying his Chicken Marsala which now that she saw it his food also looked pretty tasty. If she ever came here with Jaden she would have to order it. She was taking small bites because on the food shows she watched it supposedly helped enhance the flavor profiles and the complexity of the dish. Plus, she didn't want to risk choking on her food. Nobody looks attractive while they're turning blue or someone is giving them the Heimlich maneuver.

When the waitress came around and asked about desserts, she decided to try something called Panna Cotta which the menu described as an Italian custard dessert that's name translated to cooked cream. It was topped with berries and a caramel drizzle. Noah ordered Tiramisu which according to the menu was a layered Italian dessert with a base of ladyfingers that were soaked in coffee and had layers of mascarpone cheese and cocoa powder. When it arrived, Noah asked for an extra fork and plate then asked Lucy if she wanted to try it. She wasn't a fan of coffee, but she decided it would be polite to at least try it so she let him use the fork to cut off a small piece and put it on the extra plate. She took a bite and decided that while it was a beautiful dessert she wasn't a fan. She was however a fan of her dessert.

After they were both finished eating their desserts Lucy wondered what she was supposed to do now. Did people usually pay the bill and leave immediately after eating? Should she ask him more questions? She didn't want this date to feel like an interrogation, but she was still curious about him.

Before she could ask him another question, he reminded her it was his turn to ask a question.

"Do you believe in love at first sight?" He asked looking at her.

She thought about it carefully before answering because she didn't want to seem too cheesy or scare him off.

"I'd like to think it's possible if two people are meant for each other things will just click into place."

Noah looked like he was deep in thought about her answer. She hoped her answer wasn't too vague. It was an honest answer. She did want to believe in true love she just hadn't seen it firsthand. Her feelings for Noah were strong, but she wasn't sure it was love. If it was, did he feel the same way. She decided to ask him the same question.

"Noah, do you believe in love at first sight?"

Now he was the one that looked like he was trying to choose his words carefully.

" Yes, I believe that it happens when you meet a person and it feels as though you have met them before. While it may seem confusing to feel such intense emotions for someone you just met there is an instant sense of euphoria that you get when you see them. You look into their eyes and visualize spending an eternity with them. It goes beyond a physical attraction. It's like two halves of a whole finding one another."

Lucy twirled a piece of hair in her finger as she prepared to ask him the next question.

"Uh.I.Umm I.. don't really know how to ask this without making you uncomfortable, but uh..hmm... how important is physical intimacy in a relationship to you?"

Her cheeks turned a light pinkish red as her eyes shifted down and she fiddled with her hands underneath the table. Her mind was racing, growing more worried every second that went by. What if he thought she was asking because she was repulsed by the idea of physical intimacy. Or worse what if he thought she assumed he was only interested in physical intimacy with her. She had regretted the question instantly but there was no turning back now. The words had been spoken. The ball was in his court. She forced herself to look up at him hoping that she could decipher any clues or emotions.

He moved swiftly into the seat beside her and gently placed his hand against her cheek moving it lightly across like the touch of a feather. Her body trembled against his hand in response as a shiver traveled down her spine. He removed his hand from her cheek and took her hand in his and began speaking.

"Min älskling, don't be embarrassed. I did not find your question to be intrusive. It would be dishonest of me to say that I do not place any importance on physical intimacy in a relationship. I have indulged in such pleasures of the flesh in the past. However, I do not find it to be the most important aspect of a relationship. Call me old fashioned, but I would never pressure you into a situation in which you are uncomfortable or not ready for. I cannot lie, the thought of being intertwined in sheer ecstasy with you would be a most pleasant one. Were you to ask me to take you home and make love to you at this very moment I would happily oblige your request. Please do not take this as an insult, but I could tell by the hesitation in your voice when you asked the question that you are worried that I would see your lack of experience as a weakness. Do not let this thought trouble you any further I want to let things progress as fast or slow as you want them to. Trust me when I say I want more than your body, of which I find quite heavenly. I want an emotional connection, honest open communication, and most importantly I want whatever you are willing to give me for however much time we have together."

A sense of relief washed over her as she let out a relaxed breath as she processed everything, he had just told her.

He wanted all of her, not just her body and it felt nice to be wanted. She felt a strange sense of comfort with him being so close to her. Could this actually be what falling in love at first sight felt like? Was this what people meant when they said they had found their soulmate?

She still wasn't 100% sure of either of those things existed but she was willing to take the chance that one or both of them did. That was enough questions for tonight. From the sounds of it she would have much more time to get to know him.

When the waitress came around again inquiring about the bill, he pulled out his wallet to pay. For what it was worth she had been in the process of pulling her money out, but he had insisted on paying. When they got back out to his car, just as before he opened the door for her and she climbed in. On the drive back home, she stared out at the starry night aimlessly in thought and bliss.

When he pulled into her apartment complex and went to open up her door she took the opportunity of his face being closer to eye level and spontaneously kissed him. He was taken aback by this, but he didn't resist. Instead, he helped her out of the car and shut the door. He placed his hands near her hips gently guiding her back until she was up against the car door.

He leaned down, tilted his head, and pressed his lips against hers. As their lips locked an electric current surged through her body ignited by the closeness of their bodies. He cupped one of his hands underneath her chin and the other against the nape of her neck frantically kissing her like a silent plea, desperate for her permission to give into desire, but with a hint of restraint. Her heart was beating in her chest her breathing irregular. He pulled back slowly his hand sliding from her neck and down to her lower back. This gave her time for her breathing to return to normal.

Her lips were tingling and her cheeks felt warm. She playfully traced her finger from his neck and down his side. As she did this, he made a pleased hum sound through his lips. He pressed his forehead to hers and in a hushed tone uttered a four-letter word that began with an f and ended with a k. He moved back and allowed her to step away from the door. The corners of his lips turned up as a smile crept across his face and then he began to speak.

"Miss Lofthouse, I really must go now before I let my primal urges take over and beg you to allow me into your home. At which point I would then scoop you up into my arms, carry you into your bedroom, and with your permission have my wicked way with you."

She hadn't intended for things to get so intense, but she couldn't say she regretted it either. She had to admit his unabashed honesty was something she liked about him. He wasn't interested in playing games. Not mind games anyways. She had a feeling if she offered, he had a few others he'd like to play. She let him walk her to her door and went inside. When she was sure that he pulled far enough away she did a little happy dance like a football player who had just scored the game winning touchdown.

She brought two fingers to her lips tracing them lightly, brushing them with a gentle touch of her fingertips. A smile started to form as she remembered the lovely tingling sensation she had felt upon her lips just mere minutes ago, a lingering reminder of unbridled passion. Admittedly the desire to throw caution to the wind and give into temptation had crossed her mind for a fleeting moment. This notion was foreign to her, she had always been so shy and reserved moving through life just existing. Being in Noah's presence had awakened and stirred up feelings of excitement and the possibility of living life to the fullest. There was plenty of time later to think about the trajectory of this new relationship moving forward. Right now, it was late and she needed to take a shower and get ready for bed.

Chapter Seventeen:

Fallout of the Date

Concentrating at work the next day was a difficult task, she couldn't wait to ask Jaden to come over later so she could tell him all about her date. Her day was long and filled with the same routine as always. Help customers, fold shirts, wipe everything down with a rag, and hope that she'd make it through the day without any issues. Rinse and repeat.

So far there hadn't been any issues. With the amount of guests in house everyday items had quite literally been flying off the shelf. Last week Matt had stopped by and informed her that the shop had made $3,000 in a single day.

She was standing at her register minding her own business when a guy came up to the register and completely unprompted started telling her about his lady friend upstairs. Weirdly the details did not stop there. By the time he finished talking she had heard all about them being in a long distance relationship for three years and how she had traveled from two states away to meet him in real life. Then he went into further very specific detail about how she was unimpressed with how small he was in the downstairs area. He followed that little detail up by informing her that he made it up in other ways though and proceeded to give her a visual via a crude motion of wiggling his tongue in between his fingers while winking.

Luckily before he could give further details his lady friend came around the corner and told him to stop being inappropriate especially to a cashier who was probably underage. At that exact moment she thanked her lucky stars that apparently, she could still pass for a high school student. Sometimes it bothered her that people thought she was younger because irate customers would talk to her as if she was a child. Today however, in the presence of a stranger giving way too much information about personal bedroom business she'd let them assume she was too young.

The things people felt comfortable sharing with complete strangers was baffling sometimes. Once she had opened up the gift shop and found a note on the counter from the night before. In the note the guest had left there was a room number and an invitation for the nighttime cashier to come up to his room for a hookup. Almost every employee had crazy guest stories. Some of the stories would start out perfectly normal and then end with insane plot twists. For instance, a lady had called downstairs in the middle of the night asking for more towels. Completely normal request. In contrast, whenever Eli, the night auditor took them upstairs the lady answered the door wearing nothing but a smile.

A couple of nights later she finally got the chance to tell Jaden about her date. He was sitting on the opposite end of her couch drinking a Dr. Crush and listening intently. She thought his eyes were going to pop out of his head when she described how the night had ended. He was surprised, but supportive that she was exploring the possibilities of having a little fun in this newly formed relationship. It was nice to know that Jaden didn't think she was acting too impulsively.

Now that he had heard the entire story he was asking her more on depth questions. "How would you rate his kissing skills on a scale of 1 to 10? 1 being "absolutely awful" and 10 being "foot lifting mind-blowingly amazing?"

Unsurprisingly it didn't take long for her to come up with an answer. "I'd definitely go with a 10. When his luscious lips pressed against mine, I felt like I was being lifted to the heavens and floating among the stars."

After hearing her description Jaden sat there in silence contemplating what he could possibly respond back to her comment.

"Hmm...I need to find a man like that. Like right now. Do you think Build-A-Boy has any guys like him in stock? The last guy I kissed talked way too much. I had to take my hand and snap his lips shut. He was killing the vibe."

That last comment had them both roaring with laughter. Build A Boy. The hand over some poor guy's lips. She was picturing Jaden in the guy's living room. Mid make out session. Then the guy goes to speak and all of a sudden Jaden's hand flies in like a Venus Fly Trap. Tears were forming at the corner of her eyes now and her sides were starting to hurt. Jaden just shrugged and said it was like that sometimes.

"When do you think you're going to see him again? Did he say he'd call you or did you leave him too hot under the collar to think straight?"

Huh she hadn't thought about that. Was she waiting for him to call, or was she supposed to reach out to him again?

Guess she'd just have to wait and see. He had implied that he wanted to see her again. Either way she was right in the middle of giving Jaden an answer when they heard a knock on her door.

Well, that was strange. The only visitor she ever had was Jaden, and he was sitting in the same room as her. She opened the door to find a delivery man holding a large vase filled with a mixture of orange and dark pink roses. After giving her signature to acknowledge that she had received them she closed the door and took them to the counter to see if there was a card to indicate who they were from. Jaden had gotten up from the couch to come stand beside her. He was just as curious as her. She found the card and started to read it.

Lucy,

My little light in a world of darkness,

your radiance outshines even these flowers.

Since the first time I laid eyes upon you I have been fascinated by your beauty.

I am eternally grateful that you walked into my establishment that night.

I will call upon you soon to set up another date.

Thinking of you fondly,

Noah

As she read the note she felt like thousands of tiny butterflies were fluttering their wings in her stomach. These roses were beautiful, and expensive but he had felt she was worth the cost. Squee! He had written that he was going to call her soon to set up another date. Until now she had only hoped and dreamed of the day when a guy would come into her life and want to spend the rest of his life with her. There was more to him than being a drop-dead gorgeous casino owner, and she was eager to find out everything she could about him.

She had always heard that different colored roses had meanings. She wondered what the symbolism was for orange and dark pink. It felt far too coincidental for him to have randomly picked out these two colors. From various searches she concluded that orange roses were synonymous with fascination, desire, and enthusiasm. The dark pink roses were a sign of appreciation and gratitude. Based upon what he had written these two colors had been chosen with intent. A smile spread across her face at the thought of him taking the time out of his busy schedule to pick out these roses while thinking to himself that she would look it up.

Jaden hadn't said anything but she knew he was dying to make a comment. After all it wasn't like getting flowers was a regular occurrence for her.

"Look at you getting flowers from a man. You got him wrapped around your finger. I better be the best man at y'all's wedding."

Then he looked at his phone and said he had to get back to his apartment.

"Well, it's been an eventful day, but I think I'm going to get out of here in case he calls. Keep me posted. "

After Jaden left, she relaxed on the couch and watched a few episodes of Ruthless Kitchen and then got up to make a quick dinner and returned to the couch. She was lying there still thinking about the flowers when her phone rang. She grabbed it off the table and looked at the caller ID to see that it said "Noah's Office." When he said soon, he actually meant soon. From the shows she watched and the way people she worked with talked when a guy said he'd call you "soon" that could mean one hour, one day, or 7-14 business days. The latter was usually referred to as "soft ghosting".

A person being completely "ghosted" meant the person would up and disappear without a trace forever. Soft ghosting meant the person wanted to see you again at some point but time was not of essence. After she let it ring three times she answered. Might as well keep him on his toes a little. She answered in a honeyed tone that was so sweet it could give a person a cavity and only said two words.

"Hello Noah,"

She heard a sound like a low throaty rumble on the other end and then he began speaking "Did you receive the flowers I sent you?"

She thought about how to answer without sounding like a high school girl whose boyfriend had just asked her to go to homecoming. She could compliment them and then make a joke to see how he'd respond.

"Yes, thank you, they arrived earlier and they were lovely, however my favorite roses are lavender." She certainly was not expecting him to respond with what he said next."

Well, hjärtanskär, it seems as though I will have to send you another bouquet tomorrow now that I am aware of this."

She knew she had to end this joke now or he'd probably send her two lavender bouquets tomorrow. After he'd already spent enough money on the first bouquet. It's not as if he was going to go broke overnight by sending her flowers, but that wasn't the point. She didn't want him to think that she enjoyed him frivolously spending money on her either.

"Uh Noah please don't do that. I was just joking. I adore the ones you sent today. I'm sure you put a lot of thought into them. I appreciate the card too."

She heard a chuckle on the other end of the phone and then his hypnotizing voice." It seems as though I was correct in assuming that you would look up the meaning of the roses. This brings me immense pleasure. The taste of your lips has been on my mind since last night."

Good god! This man knew exactly how to push her buttons. He should be getting paid overtime for the amount of work he was putting in. Speaking of work, she was distracted by the thought of him sitting in his office wearing a suit leaning back in one of those high-backed chairs his feet propped up on the desk one arm folded behind his neck. She really needed to focus on this conversation instead of daydreaming. She already did more than enough dreaming about him at night. Not that it bothered her as much anymore since he had mutual feelings. It would still be embarrassing if he found out about them though. Yeah, she was definitely not going to ever tell him about them. She was brought back to reality by a chuckling noise on the other end. Wait, what had he just said? Now she was going to have to ask him to repeat what he said. It totally wasn't going to seem like she had gotten distracted by his voice or what he said at all. Reluctantly she asked him to start over.

"Why Miss Lofthouse, were you thinking about me just now? If you were I hope they were only good thoughts. Actually, I take that back you can throw in a few naughty ones if you wish." It was a good thing he couldn't see her look of embarrassment through the phone.

Although she had a feeling that wasn't what he had actually said when she hadn't been listening. Especially since he had emitted a hearty laugh right after he said it.

He really enjoyed getting her flustered. "As I was saying, at your earliest convenience I would like to take you out again."

She didn't want to keep him waiting too long. He did have other business to attend to. Or at least she thought he did.

He was the owner after all, obviously if he wanted to make personal calls there were other people who kept the place running. Though she did like the thought of him making time just for her.

"Well, I have next Wednesday and Thursday off so whichever day works for you. If either of those works for you. I don't really know your schedule or anything, but if neither does you can choose the day." She hoped one of those days worked for him as well, but if they didn't it's not like she was going to turn him down.

If it was a day she worked she'd just have to go to work tired the next day if they were going to be out late. A good relationship was built on compromise, or so she'd heard.

"Then I shall pick you up next Wednesday at 7pm sharp. I will be looking forward to it all week. As satisfying as it would be to speak to you all night, I must get off the phone now. Sorry, casino business to attend to. Godnatt, Lucy. Sweet dreams Miss Lofthouse."

His voice became lower and flirty as he said the last part. She was seriously starting to think he might actually be psychic. Did he somehow know that she had been dreaming of him? Then again it was a common phrase. It was also nighttime and people usually started preparing for bed soon. It was also possible he just liked the idea of her dreaming about him. I mean he had joked about her thinking of him. At least she thought it he said it as a joke, but what if he was being completely serious. He had already admitted to thinking of her. It was no secret that she didn't have enough relationship experience to know how much she was supposed to be thinking of him. Well two could play this game. If he wanted her thinking of him, she'd give him something to think about.

In the flirtiest voice she could think of she responded back. "Good night Mr. Eastman."

Then she hung up the phone. After that she continued with her usual nighttime routine. She showered, put on a pair of pajamas with the sun and stars on them, brushed her teeth and then laid down in bed.

Chapter Eighteen:

Dreamin Big

"Level with me Doll, is this automobile the bees' knees or what?"

"It's swell, Baby"

When your fella is a big shot, he can afford a breezer like the 1925 Silver Phantom that boasts having a big six, 4 speed gearbox that achieves 40/50 horsepower and has custom leather seats that are fit for king (and his queen!). Why the salesman even said it can reach top speeds of 80 miles per hour. If anyone is going to drive that fast it's my fella. It's quiet as a Phantom to boot! The quietest in all the world according to all the advertisements.

"Hawt Dawg! This breezer cost a lot of clams, but anything my dame wants she gets " he said with a laugh.

Tonight, my fella sure is looking dapper in his black suit with his dark blonde hair reminiscent of the wheat fields and his blue eyes that sparkle like the ocean on a summer's day. He's a big shot who runs the Moonlight Mischief, the Speakeasy we're headed to. In fact, he's one of the most well-known bootleggers in all of New York City.

People from all over come to our establishment to let loose and cut a rug while indulging in Giggle Water and Moonshine. Since Prohibition banned libations several years ago, the flat foots have shut down almost every other Gin Mill and sent all the owners to the big house. Moonlight Mischief is well hidden being underground and all. But my fella says if we're ever discovered we'll just go on the lam and open up another one somewhere else.

He tells me not to worry about such notions tonight because we're having a celebration. We finally went down the aisle! That's why I'm all dolled up in my wedding dress and wearing the brand-new gold ring that my fella gave me. This new car was his gift to me. I tell him all the time that his love is enough, but I have to admit this car is the cat's meow. It was a lot of dough, but he says no dame of his will be seen riding around in a jalopey.

As we zoom past all the big city lights and tall buildings it's a reminder that we live in the city that never sleeps. This works out well for a couple of night owls like us though. I don't mind at all living amongst the moon and the stars with my fella. I'd do anything for him and vice versa. Theres nothing like beholding the sight of thousands of lights twinkling and gleaming everywhere you look. Well except for looking at my fella right now, but that's what happens when you're goofy for each other.

"Get a wiggle on," my fella playfully says to me as he swats at my behind when we get out of the vehicle which is now parked in front of the hotel that is a hidden front for our secret speak easy.

During the day the hotel is on the up and up so the flatfoots are none the wiser about the secret night time festivities. The entrance is behind a hidden door in the basement. Since my fella is the owner, we don't have to use cards or a password to get in. However, he did let me pick the password which is "Enchanted Moonlight Serenade. "

Once we enter, I look around at the rich dark wood paneling, and couches with dark red velvet couches. Vintage chandeliers provide low lighting that casts a warm glow over the room which is perfect for having intimate conversations or necking for those feeling more risqué. The sound of Jazz Music resonates throughout the room vibrant and energetic to inspire folks to cut a rug on the dance floor. The dance floor is filled with Flappers doing their sultry Shimmy dances in their beautiful beaded dresses, feathered headbands, and Mary Janes. Others are wearing sequined dresses with rhinestone headbands and T-Strap shoes.

Fast paced music inspires people with a carefree and rebellious spirit to swing their arms and twist their bodies in time with the lively and energized beats. When the music slows down couples often do The Fox Trot. Gliding along smoothly, spinning and twirling gracefully in perfect harmony to the romantic and slow-paced tunes. During one of those romantic songs, he pulls me in closer and whispers in my ear, professing his undying love to me. I am already well aware of this as he spoke these same words during our vows, but it's still pretty swell to hear. He kisses my neck tenderly afterwards which he knows I particularly enjoy even if we are in a room full of people.

The commotion of two people shouting nearby fills the air and then I hear a loud popping sound. The music comes to a screeching halt and then people start running towards the exit.

Mere moments later I notice the pain radiating from my abdomen. I look down and a dark red spot has started to form and grow larger with every "thump thump" of my heartbeat. He holds onto me trying to keep me steady as I feel myself grow weaker. He's trying to put on a brave face for me, but I can see the tears forming in the corners of his eyes as the blood is now gushing out of me like a waterfall.

He scoops me into his strong arms and carries me over to the countertop and gently places me flat on my back. He grabs a rag and places it over the spot firmly, but gently applying pressure to try to stop the bleeding. We both know that it's futile because I've already lost so much blood. Regardless, I know he's still going to try. He pauses for a moment and embraces me placing a tender kiss on my lips. Before I lose the last of my remaining strength I manage to whisper "I love you". As my eyes start to shut and I feel myself drift into unconsciousness I can feel him place his hand upon mine. As my hearing starts to fade the last thing I hear him say is "death is not the end, my love. We will find each other again in your next life."

Beep-Beep! Beep-Beep! She slowly opened her eyes groggily reaching over with one arm to turn the alarm off. She couldn't remember the entire dream, only bits and pieces here and there, but the last words were still swimming around in her mind. A single tear slid down her cheek. This latest dream was far from the other dreams in which she usually imagined herself and Noah.

Even though it was just a dream she felt a deep sense of sadness for some reason. Although she supposed that was normal when you have a dream about love ending in such a tragic way. At the same time there was a hint of optimism in his voice as he said that they would reunite in another life. If there was such a thing as soulmates, was it really such a stretch to believe that love could be powerful enough for two people to find each other in another life? There was plenty of time to worry about that later though, right now it was time for her to climb out of bed and start getting ready for work.

Made in the USA
Columbia, SC
08 June 2025

59066248R00112